The D

By Eric

ISBN 978-1-7333264-7-6

Third Edition

CHI MEDIA
COMPANY

For Benjamin,
to whom I had the privilege of giving life.

TABLE OF CONTENTS

One

From NEW YORK DAILY (*10/7/11*):

Unique to this case is the fact that the suicidal planning of the sect has been foreseen and predicted, but has not yet been confirmed.

Says Jed Bracken, a former member, "I was in it for five years, just about. Initially, it wasn't anything controversial. It was more fun. You get rid of the material life. Get rid of goals. Get rid of conformity, being tied down to your job and that sort of thing. And he took care of us, and I'd have to say with sincerity that most of us were probably very happy.

"But the concept of what he called 'Ascension' began to creep into the things he talked about. Ascension basically meant taking your own life. Because as far as he was concerned, your consciousness wasn't really real. If you got to the core of it, you were left with sort of an empty hum. And that to him was the realest thing."

Mr. Bracken then went on to explain that although Mr. Pike described Ascension as the ultimate parting with the delusions of this world, neither he nor many other members were interested in following that path.

"The ones who went with him, yes. They were hardcore. We're talking hours of meditation every day. To the point where you're just kind of floating instead of living. Most of us, though, weren't really down with his message. We preferred to exist here; we didn't see a need for that next step. And frankly, if you want my opinion, if he manages to take those eight people with him when he goes, it won't be any kind of spiritual advancement. It'll be a f-cking execution."

Two

Summerland, CA
11/11/11 (Last Day)
Matthew Barrett's Mind
2:02AM

The Leader was right. No surprise there.

When I wake, I don't feel as though I'm in a room.

That was His intention.

Upon our arrival at this house, He said that it was time to Ascend to a new level. During the days leading up to our final Ascension, we would transition from a life of the minimal to a life of the elemental. These were His words, and to be honest I'm suspicious as to whether there's a true distinction. In any case, I get His meaning...

It was time to transition from a life of very few material things to a life of next to no material things. Back there, in the mansion, we had our regular clothes and our books and our films and musical instruments. Some of us even had our cars. Cell phones, also, though we used them less and less as we all grew closer.

Here, however, it's a new order. Our own things are gone. We all wear white garbs, and sometimes the women wear nothing at all. Sometimes Theodore, too, elects to wear nothing at all, which makes me feel a certain way, not positive.

In any case: The Leader pointed out to me – maybe in the first week we knew each other – that all of society is structured in the form of boxes, both physical and symbolic.

Our homes are boxes.

Our cars are boxes.

Where we work, boxes.

And then there's the non-physical, the labels people put on us. Your parents were Republicans, so you must be a Republican. Your best friend fucked a girl with herpes, so your dick must leak, also.

But there are no boxes in this house.

Sure, it's a house like any other – it isn't in the shape of a circle or something – but the lack of furniture and decorations makes it feel more fluid. You can stare at the walls and get absorbed into them.

And when I wake, given the fact that it's just me and a mattress and Jolie in here, I don't feel as though I'm in a room. I'm free.

That's the whole point. It's not complicated. It's all about what He calls "the gush." It's inside of all of us, but most of us constrict it. It's the overflow of all that you are. Your instincts, feelings, spirit – the *gush. Let it out*. Meditation can help. It rakes away the conscious chatter.

That's what we did: raked it away.

But now--

This is strange.

I'd like to gush right out the door. And my heart is really beating...

I hug Jolie. A special privilege, she is. Most of us don't travel in pairs. The Leader, however, saw our special love.

Three

From private correspondence to Matthew Barrett from his brother, Derrick Barrett (*9/1/11*):

Dude, you taught me like everything I know. Since you've been away I realized I haven't been learning very much anymore which is sad. Like talking about the universe. You were always the smartest and our whole family knew it. So I don't want to believe that you're running around with a phony guy who puts ideas in your head. Cuz that head is too good and we need it. I know the world isn't the warmest place and I don't expect it to be but I expect we can each do what we can to make it better instead of running away from it. And I'm sorry to say that that's what everybody around here is starting to say that you did.

Four

Last Day – 3:47AM

I wake again.

And my sleep since the last time I woke wasn't real sleep. It was all bending shapes and forward-arching walls. And within all that, something really fucked-up happened.

A phone rang.

I prop myself up on my elbows. No sooner do I complete the action than I regret it, for it's a sign of panic.

Why did I hear a ringing phone?

Day one, all of our phones got stripped. None of us knows exactly where they are, but I know Him well enough to know that they're probably in the drawer in the nightstand beside His bed. He's the only one with a nightstand, you see, and He wouldn't bother with it if it didn't lend utility.

So I'm guessing the phones are there, but come on, they're off. He probably even took out the batteries.

And there's no land line in the house, that I know for sure.

Yet, crisp and hard and rolling my way, that was a fucking ring.

I sit up now. More regret; more proof of panic. Jolie's still asleep, doesn't even stir. I look around at the darkness, regarding with irony that if the light were turned on, my visual terrain would be just as smooth, only instead of black it would be made of white.

Hold on. Go slow. You didn't hear a phone.

It was just a dream.

Even though you weren't really sleeping.

I'm fucked. I get up. My goddamn heart. My body, naked, draws in the cold.

I'd like to leave our room and investigate, but the mere thought soaks me through with terror. What if I saw Him in the hall? Tiptoe as soft as possible, He'd still very possibly hear me.

I couldn't bear to hear Him yell. My tongue is...nothing. It doesn't work. It's like my heart's sending blood everywhere but it.

"Did you hear something?" I ask Jolie.

One more night of sleep on this Earth, and due to me, it'll now have a break in it. But on the other hand, when woken up, she's always easy.

This girl, I love.

Her honey skin. Her exotic origins: Africa, Asia, a little Native American. Like twelve percent white, I believe.

She, like me, is up now, though a good deal less so. She's still down in the slumber weeds, face kissed cool by soil.

But she goes, "Hmm?"

"Did you hear that? It was like a...telephone ringing."

Now her eyelids flutter a little.

"What're-you-talking-about?"

Did I just...actually hear it again?

No, that's bullshit. If I did, it was like a hundred times lower. It was more like my memory of the first one than a legitimate second one. A weird, floating, out-of-head memory, but still.

"Huh?" she asks.

"Sssshhh," I say, a vertical digit at my lips, as I'm now apparently unsure if that was a memory.

But now she's more awake. Paradoxes everywhere; another lesson from Him. You want the girl to talk, she's asleep. You want the girl to shush, she sits up on her elbow.

"We have no phone," she explains, a fact so known it's not worth the crutch of words. "It was a dream, baby. Come back."

"Was weird," I say, when the fact is it continues to be so.

My unseeing eyes look around.

"No, come on," she says. "Come back to bed."

"I feel like going outside."

This isn't right. It's dissent.

Or worse.

One more step in that direction, and we're talking about revolt.

"Huh? What?" she asks, and the two words sound like parts of one: *Huhwhat*?

I'm a man at a fork. A boy, really. Only twenty-six trips 'round the sun. To my left is outside: grass, air, mystery. To my right is inside: bed, Jolie...

And more panic, probably.

A bed to a panicked person is like quicksand to a fish: It works in the broadest, most half-minded strokes, but functions as a disaster in reality.

"I have to go," I say. "We should walk on the grass together. You want to?"

And now I've painted her onto the canvas. The idea of her coming makes the whole thing seem rosy. Walking. Trading stares. The creep of the night. There must be a psychological term for that: dragging somebody with you on a mission that you're only half-sure of, and thus getting yourself closer to sureness.

Her body, however, makes me think of quicksand again. It sinks its way deeper into the mattress. More words come from her, but they've got her pillow to contest with: "You crazy? He wants us inside."

Another plain fact. A corpse, upon hearing it, would roll his eyes. But so what? Are we abandoning Him?

Are we at all like the others? The ones who ran?

"Just for a minute," I say.

But those words, I'm reasonably certain, go unheard. She's asleep again, on the other side of my inflicted break.

Five

From BREAKING NEWS L.A. (*10/4/11*):

Although police have pressed a variety of charges against Mr. Pike relating to his alleged sexual assault of the two female members and his alleged child endangerment of the infant, Victor Garcia, as of yet no kidnapping charges have been filed.

"To the best of our understanding," said Santa Barbara District Attorney Peter Francis, "these followers went with him voluntarily. They were not taken by force, whatever the claims of the followers who chose not to stay."

When asked if police officials had any clues as to The Missing Nine's whereabouts, Francis said that their location was unknown, but that Mr. Pike was thought to have sufficient financial resources to rent a home, and was more than likely still in the Southern California area. A Santa Barbara resident for more than twenty years, he was not thought to have connections out of state, nor an established propensity for travel.

Six

Last Day – 3:59AM

Unclothed. A bare boy. Walking on the grass.

I think thoughts that would please Him. It's like He's here, in fact. Thinking about the myth of time. About nonconformity. The gush.

It's not all dry, though. The media makes Him out to be that way. A cardboard cut-out. He's fun, though, too. He likes cartoons and puns and discussing flatulence. There's a subtle air of raunchiness about Him, amidst the prevailing charisma and handsomeness.

And He likes fucking, also. Which is what got Him/us in so much trouble.

Never Jolie, per the terms of our agreement, but certainly many of the other members. Only girls; He swings one way.

And I sometimes wonder what happened in that room.

Before the door-slam that lit up my blood. Before the two of them ran out with mascara down their cheeks.

Did He get too rough?

I look up at the house. Up there, eight beautiful souls at rest. Him chief among them, at the end of the hall.

This night. Such a sweetness. Somewhere on the hard-on verge between pain and tenderness.

I love Him. Her, also. For them, I will do this.

And for me.

Seven

From PUBLIC FORUM TELEVISION's interview with Dr. Barry Blumenfeld (10/20/11):

PFT: You've conducted studies of all nine members.

BB: I have.

PFT: And what conclusions have you drawn? Are they brainwashed?

BB: "Brainwashing" is something of a mythical concept, the idea that you can erase what's in a person's mind. You can't, really. But what you can do is deaden the mind. Certainly. You provide low amounts of nutrients. Perhaps even narcotics. You regulate exposure to pop culture, television, books. You make the mind controllable. It's not about eliminating the contents, or "washing" them somehow.

PFT: What can you tell us, specifically, about this group?

BB: As a group or as individuals?

PFT: Both.

BB: As a group, they're intimate, certainly. Freely sexual with each other. Multiple partners. They take meals together. They labor together. So in terms of the Ascension concept, they're sort of bound by a herd mentality.

PFT: Which Edgar Pike needs to carry off the mission?

BB: Most probably, yes. He's grandiose in his thinking, Pike. Everything must be exaggerated. He can't tolerate ordinary emotions or experiences.

PFT: Manic-depressive, you'd say?

BB: Bipolar, we use. Yes, I would venture that. More manic than depressive. Gives grand speeches. Loves to talk, hear himself talk. So to kill himself, which would be a viable option given the charges against him, requires grandeur. It has to be a show. A ritual. To satisfy his ego. It can't be done in a closet, you see.

PFT: Has to be of a certain proportion...

BB: Yes, a God-like proportion. His ideal, I'm sure, would have been for all sixty members to do it, but thankfully he lost most of them.

PFT: And the others?

BB: The other eight I can put into two classifications. We can lift from Nietzsche's language, call them masters or slaves. The masters are like Edgar Pike. They want grandeur. Beth McKay goes in this category. An actress. Jolie True, also. Artistic talent there. With Matthew Barrett, there's more of an introverted psyche, but he enjoys power. Pike gives it to him, calls him an assistant. It gives Matthew meaning. Hard to let go of.

PFT: Even if it means your death...

BB: Even if it means your death. Theodore Hall is a diagnosed schizophrenic. Massive perceptual difficulty is indicated there. And grandiose, very often. The others – Michael Graves, Susan Hynes –

PFT: Paul Laundry...

BB: Paul Laundry and Cathleen Carnevale. These individuals are in a more normative perceptual category. I call them "slaves" only as a categorization.

PFT: Well, the whole group is enslaved...

BB: Yes, essentially. Though this latter segment isn't trading on the drama. The ritual aspect doesn't move them. They're left-brained: they follow the ritual without getting emotional about it. They know the steps. They know the schedule. It's straight and narrow.

PFT: Is there any chance at all of an aborted ritual? Somebody coming to their senses?

BB: In my judgment, I'd say no.

PFT: "No."

BB: Because we're dealing with humans who've been depleted of their identities.

PFT: No doubt the cult members' families are watching this. And no doubt they're extremely concerned...

BB: Yes.

PFT: Is there any "best case scenario" whatsoever that you can propose?

BB: The flat answer is still no. It would seem that their destiny has been scheduled and sealed. If there's any chance of any member "coming to their senses," as you say...

PFT: Go on...

BB: This is purely speculative. It's not intended to raise expectations.

PFT: That's understood. Of course.

BB: The sole candidate who could orchestrate a "revolt," if you will, is Matthew Barrett. That's because of the hierarchical position we discussed. He does have a measure of power, which means Pike trusts him and will listen to him. But for Matthew to take any action whatsoever would require him to in no way be suicidal, which the evidence does not support. The evidence tells us that Matthew was estranged from his family and living on the street when Pike befriended him years ago. This is not a young man with very many viable prospects, in other words.

PFT: Not much sense of a future.

BB: Most likely, no.

Eight

Last Day – 6:00AM: RISE

We fucked. I hope not for the last time.

It's six, which gives us twelve more hours. We'll find time for more. He encourages it.

Here, you can say how good your morning come-shot was, and you'll get a smile of support. Maybe even get asked for details. Find yourself going on about textures, comparing feelings to foods.

I hoped, as we fucked, to channel all my fear into my come, thereby giving it a way out. Not into her – getting her pregnant now is one paradox we can do without – but on her ass. I looked at it and hoped I saw my fear gone from me.

It sort of worked. Hard to say yet. I'm all adrenal now. The sun's up. Everything's speeding at a faster clip.

Right before six, He knocked on our door. Us first, before the other six rooms. A privilege of being second in charge.

This time (the last time), when I woke, there was no ringing phone. There was just Him, in the doorway, catching sunshine from the curtain-less window. The window alone breaks the white with a shock of green. We're on two acres here, though it's not hard to slip into imagining that the yard goes on forever.

We made eye contact. That I love; the shot it gives me.

"Get up," He said. "The sun's bursting!"

Nine

From BREAKING NEWS L.A.'s exclusive interview with Anonymous (10/5/11):

It was his kindness that kept the machine running. However, there could be no mistaking that it was a machine. There were chores. Every day involved a rigorous schedule. Up at the same time. Cleaning the same rooms, same floors. Very organized, with Edgar and Jed at the top.

This was intended to get us out of ourselves. To him, everything we thought of as "ourselves" was B.S. It didn't matter that I had earned a Master's Degree, or that I had a daughter who'd passed away from asthma. Our personal narratives were looked at as disposable.

Which was just as well, since we wanted so very badly to forget.

But our bodies were another story. The bodies were valuable. It got to a point where only good-looking people were admitted into the home. Some early members didn't have to meet that standard, but for the most part it was very obvious that we were being...cast, in a way. It wasn't based on our spiritual understanding.

It was based on how badly he wanted to make love to us.

Ten

Last Day – 6:15AM: EMBRACE

Now it's all of us on the back lawn.

Me and Jolie. Michael and Paul. Theodore. Susan, Cathleen, and Beth.

All of us beautiful, I can only think. Myself included. Many would call that ego; I call it valuing the self. The Leader does, also.

We hug.

In rotation. All of us hug all of us. There's no time limit.

Which is just as well, for there is no time.

Oftentimes, when paired, Jolie and I rush through it. Feel a little silly about hugging in front of the others. Too plain, given the preexisting obviousness of our pairing.

Today, though, we let our hug go on. Let it advance from a hug into a melt.

When I hug Beth, she cries. I feel her wetness on my own cheek. And then, sneaking up on myself, I cry, also.

Eleven

Last Day – 6:30AM: EXERCISE

Five push-ups, followed by five jumping-jacks.

On the ground, then – *strain*! – back up.

It's not for our bodies. Sure, they receive some collateral help, but they're soon to expire, alas.

It's for our minds. Endorphins. A gush, if you will. Keep that sweet juice throbbing all the live long day.

Five down/five up.

Twelve

Last Day – 7:00AM: TAI CHI

Tai Chi's for the breath. It befriends the lungs. Bronchial tubes take leave of their industrialized, 21st-century tension.

Everything a flow.

The Leader joins us for these each day. For here He must actually lead each time. The moves bear rhythm, and they take on contorted shapes.

All of us not in sync any longer, as we were with the push-ups and the jacks.

Now it's freedom. Origami made human.

The grass and our bare feet in love.

Thirteen

Last Day –7:45AM: JOG

Only I have stopped.

The jogging, that is. The seven others jog around the lawn. Jolie sometimes waves when she passes.

The Leader smiles at me, touches my shoulder, which is moving up and down on account of my breath.

I look around. My skull feels blown open. All this space. Not one neighboring home, just some dashes of woods.

Sunlight sparkling through in a weirdo giggle.

"The day has to go quickly," The Leader says, and even though He called me over, I'm still surprised that He's addressing me.

The Leader turns from them to me. His face now mine. "It has to go quickly because they'll want it to go slowly."

I look down, the tissue surrounding my eyes pulled taut in a squint. I have to actually ponder His words. Simple, yes, but are they true? Will all of us desire slowness? Maybe we'll want to get it over with, like pulling a band-aid off a patch of hair.

"Matthew?" He says.

Shit. He's seen me thinking. Damn flies buzzing within my head. When we talk, it's best to try to stay clean. He can see cleanliness, too, in the liquid purity of the eyes.

"They'll want it to go slowly because they'll cling to their lives. We can't let them cling too hard, or there'll be difficulties."

I still need a moment to align with His frequency. He's actually expressing that there will be resistance. Not necessarily revolt – different concept – but the basic will to live. This isn't hard for me to grasp – I'm down with dualistic concepts – yet I am surprised to hear Him being so plain.

But I'm thinking too much when talking would be appropriate. "How do we make the day go quickly?" I ask.

Bad question. Lands like a plane without wheels. He's pleased by any reply, however.

"A lot of that's gonna rest on me," He says. "I'll have to give a very good speech at breakfast. And we stick to the schedule we've always kept. Except fewer breaks this time, and less food. Keep the bodies pure, but maintain the momentum."

"Okay."

"All right," He tells me. "Go 'head."

And as though my heels have sprouted springs, I find myself returning to the jog.

Theodore eyes me as I return. Not liking the break I got. His cheeks scrunched up with sourness.

Fourteen

Poem Written By Theodore Hall (*circa 1986*):

There's a wall of blood I dream of
Coming at me like a brick
There's a wall of blood I dream of
Coming at me, never dripping
There's a wall of blood I dream of
It could cover me, cover my screams
There's a wall of blood I dream of
When my mind bleeds in my dreams
There's a wall of blood...it's staring
It wants to know my name
There's a wall of blood...I'm sharing
And I'll never be the same.

Fifteen

Last Day – 9AM: BREAKFAST

We are tired when we sit down to eat, and by "we" I do not include The Leader.

He is fresh, and standing. Six-foot-two by common measures, but tall as a mountain in here.

The dining room's where the deed shall occur. It's nine now, giving us nine more hours. Nine and nine. My head's got a swarm of dots around it.

"Before we eat," He says, "I would like to share some thoughts with you."

He expresses this as though it's revelatory, though He says something as such every single morning.

"Now," He continues, "many negative things are far away. Yes. And we try not to let those things cross our minds. But it is understood that we have left behind careers that poisoned our spirits, husbands and wives that deadened our potential, mothers and fathers with wandering hands. We left behind bureaucracy and red tape. We left behind the sharp, biting teeth of the legal system. We left behind a world that smashed into us every day with its mighty coldness. A world that was eating away at itself -- environmentally, economically, psychologically, socially, spiritually, and emotionally. That world, we can be thankful, is far away from all of us on this day."

He pauses now, and I sense Him growing taller. Larger. The energy level in the room has spiked. Pale faces we have, yet none is without some variation of a smile: smirk, grin, even smiling eyes.

"Now let me speak of another world, as well. Not the one behind us, with its coldness, but the one in front of us, with its warmth.

"You are such brave and humbling creatures. If my heart swelled any larger with pride, it would burst within my chest. For despite so much propaganda, despite so much pressure and conformity, you are taking it upon yourselves to part with the physical plane. You know, as well as I do – if not better -- that this is not where we were meant to live. That the souls within us itch and squirm, wanting always to grow and grow...until they crack out of their shells.

"You know that at six p.m. tonight, you will be releasing more than just breath, more than just blood, but furious, blinding, magical energy. Energy that will buzz and whiz around the universe. And hopefully the energy of an old being such as myself will be able to keep up with that of you all."

A sound to my right. Beth again is crying.

"For those whose minds are locked in the world behind us, this day might be committed to memory as a day devoid of beauty. But I count myself as a lucky soul, for beauty is all that I see before me, both right now and in the hours to come. So as you take in this morning's meal, think not of the wings of the butterflies in your stomachs, but of the wings soon to grow from your own backs. Tonight we soar. We soar and soar...and soar."

And now, unless I'm (again?) hallucinating, I think that I spy tears within His eyes. I've seen them before, yes, but that was different. That was after the detectives left. This, now, is passion in release.

For this man, I am certain, I would kill.

He takes a moment to catch His breath.

"I am made up of love for all of you, my friends."

Sixteen

Edgar Pike's Journal
November, 2009

I hope this isn't holiday sentimentality, but I feel the need to put into writing that I Do Love Them. Them, my mother, myself. Period. The rest of the world, it's not hatred, but it's certainly disappointment. We Can Be Better!

Even the most conformist white collar spoiled brat knows that time doesn't exist. He knows! He knows some hours feel longer than others, and that some memories from 20 years ago snap back in an instant. But what does he do? He rushes to work every day. He gets an ulcer. Poison inside.

Here, we have no poison. Here is the house where Eros lives. Thanatos, too, if you consider all the come we shed. Massacres! Massacres and holocausts of love!

Seventeen

Last Day – 9:07AM

It is then when we realize that we haven't been breathing. For all of us, at once, exhale with force.

"Now let's eat, shall we?"

His smile, ambitious, seems to stem from real deep. As He takes His own seat, we all – I'm sure – feel as though we're sitting down for the first time since jogging.

Eighteen

From BREAKING NEWS L.A.'s exclusive interview with Jed Bracken (10/12/11):

You have to understand that he was very sensitive in terms of language. That was his weapon, essentially. He wasn't much to look at; kind of a clumsy guy. Very tall, overpowering; I'll give him that. And great eyes. Symmetrical face. But not handsome. He managed to make a lot of people think he was, but that was all smoke and mirrors.

With language, he could do whatever he wanted. He could talk all all-American: "Hey buddy, thanks a million!" That kind of shit. When he worked in sales, that's what everyone responded to. Or at least enough people to keep him busy. But once our thing got going, slowly but surely, it became less goofy. Or more goofy – depending on who you ask! He got flowery, man. I tried not to let it bug me. Seemed sincere enough. But sometimes I'd stop and think to myself – This is not the guy I met when I met him.

The guy I met in Venice Beach was more modest. Commanding presence; could get you talking for hours, but not in this overheated, mythological way. That all came later. After he realized that a good amount of people were willing to listen.

Nineteen

Last Day – 9:08AM

He's looking at me. I'm now to rise. Softly – no aggression – He snaps His fingers. I'm on my feet as though pulled by strings. Over to the island at the kitchen's center. A circle of color on its surface: fruit of shrieking brightness in a pale blue bowl.

I take it.

"One apiece," He says to me as I pass the back of His head. Bald and gleaming, it's like a rock with a brain inside of it.

I go around the table, mind underwater, and pass each of my friends a piece of fruit. Susan gives her banana a look. "Is this all for now?" she asks.

A chirp in her voice, but the question bears weight.

"Yes, Susan." His answer's as fast as a thought. "We keep breakfast and lunch light today. The energy it takes to digest, we need to preserve and devote to other things."

If Susan pauses, then I don't see it. She nods her understanding, starts to peel her banana. To me, the crack of the peel sounds loud.

Twenty

From THEHEALINGMIND.NET (*10/11/11*):

My name is Lana Hynes and my sister-in-law Susan has been featured on the news a lot lately. Susan is one of the ones called The Missing Nine. When they show her picture on the news, it is of a sad woman with her hair not combed and her face very stoic-looking. My sister-in-law Susan was known to me and our whole family as a very good baker and a very good accountant. She had two cats, Sampson and Tramp, who she loved and who I know miss her. She was not a person that was not regular. And our family believes she is being mind controlled by the man Ed Pike who took them.

Twenty-One

From THEHEALINGMIND.NET Message Board (10/11/11-10/14/11):

Shinealight4410: I'm glad Lana Hynes was brave enough to present another side of this. The media is enjoyin counting down to their deaths too much.

MaryMaryP: I agree. Was good to stop and think that there's more to this than a bunch of weird people.

TedGoesUp: I'm not trying to start an argument, but they did decide to go. They are sending a message. It's about getting over death. Not taking your life so seriously. I'm sorry the poor lady's cats miss her, but we're part of a giant universe here.

Shinealight4410: TedGoesUp, I think what you're sharing is very dangerous. I think if you think it through you'll see this is a waste of life. These people are not sick. They have families who love them, cats too. I for one am not interested in whatever message they or their sick Father (the only sick one there with them) are sending.

TedGoesUp: If you think I'M dangerous, don't watch the news.

EdgarPikeForever79: LET THEM BLEED!!

Twenty-Two

Last Day – 9:09AM

“And no liquids until Downtime,” He adds. “I want to keep bathroom breaks to a minimum. We have a lot to do.”

We eat. We go slow. Not so much to savor the food as, perhaps, to grant the length of the meal normal proportions.

He doesn’t like it. I see it. No one else does.

“Go out,” He starts, but then catches Himself.

I look at Him. I know Him. He was about to disperse an order, but He sensed that it was coming out too sharp.

“Why don’t all of you,” He revises, adopting an inquisitive posture, “go out back to the patio, enjoy your meal in nature? It’ll taste better that way.”

We’re up on our feet before He says the part about taste.

Just the same, I lick the remains of my peach from my thumb and fingertips. It began to vanish at some point while I was passing out the rest.

“Can I help you with anything, Master?” Theodore asks Him on his way to the patio door.

A strange request considering that The Leader intends to sit and eat at the moment, but that would be Theodore for you.

“No, Theodore. I’ll be fine. You go enjoy yourself.”

Before he does so (or tries to), Theodore shoots me another look. Second for today. Something’s up in that unmedicated brain. The Leader flushed his pills the day before we left. Said that enough was enough already. Then smiled about the fact that flushing pills is technically disposing of hazardous waste, and probably against the law in California.

Now it's The Leader who's eyeing me.

Wants something from me.

"Come here," He says. "Let me show you something."

* * *

You have to understand some things.

Like: This is the guy who saved my life.

The man who marked the difference between oblivion and enlightenment.

The one who said the conservatives have it wrong because government, while not worth trusting, is not worth eradicating.

And the liberals have it wrong because too much government is indeed a killer (see, again, California).

And the moderates have it wrong because splitting the difference between two forms of imperfection is insane.

And the Christians have it wrong because they essentially tell moralistic fairy tales.

Add to that the Jews, with subtle variations.

And the Buddhists have it wrong because they suffer from cleverness. Too many yins and yangs, maybes and what-have-yous.

And the atheists are fucked, 'cause, come on, you're gonna tell me that our five senses give us everything?

And the nihilists are fucked 'cause that's just too easy.

And as for existentialism, it's sexy and exciting, but more of a fashion than a mentality, and forever in search of its own definition.

And those who say money doesn't buy happiness are lying.

And those who say it does are full of shit.

And tantra's a scam 'cause it's all about the body, and the body, while smart, can't be expected to outsmart the mind.

But the mind is all wrong 'cause, hell, look where it's led us...

And hell doesn't exist, that's another (grim) fairy tale.

Islam? Don't even get Him started.

And none of this means that all of the above lack all merit.

It just means that nothing really works:

Marriage: A coin toss.

The workforce: A hamster wheel.

Cars: A death trap, for our bodies as well as the sky.

Art: Diverting, but come on? These movies, do they not recede from us, always? These books – what do we retain from them?

But ignore Him, He'll tell you.

'Cause He's without alternatives.

That is, except, for the ones in the doing.

Something about action, that's what He's getting at.

"Have to gush," He likes to say sometimes.

His eyes squinting, searching, ready for the next thing.

It's all in the thrust. The charge. The gush. That doesn't mean don't think. Doesn't even mean don't think a lot.

Doesn't mean don't feel.

Nor pray, nor dream.

He doesn't rule out anything. At the same time, though, He rules out everything.

And if this sounds like dualism, you're missing the point. The point is elusive. It's not an A-B. Not an either-or. Not even an and-both.

The point, near as He can express, is action.

Charge. Pulse. Flow. Be.

And whatever prevents you from doing that, meet with doubt and skepticism, always.

* * *

So we scrub. He gave us that.

We exercise. He gave us that.

We clean throughout the day. Chores for the soul. Or – fuck the soul (what's the soul?) -- chores for the sake of doing.

On the floor. Steel wool. The cracks between the tiles. The stare emitting from your head.

Then eating: feeling the food on your tongue. Throat. Esophagus. Belly. Intestines. Dick. Ass. Pussy. Liver.

Curse words, they're not prohibited, although He doesn't use them.

One time, though.

One time He did.

* * *

We drummed.

The beach at Venice. People do this every weekend night. Until the police arrive and break it up. That sounds romantic and mythological, but it's a fact.

They drum until the police arrive.

No arrests, ever, as far as I know.

It's just a dance.

The drummers, saying, "Fuck you. We're drumming."

The police coming back with, "Yes, boys and girls. But sometimes it's time to go home."

Everyone half-winking as it goes down.

The word was sort of out by then. Our group was known around Southern California. Not because any crimes had been reported, but because that's what happens when people talk to people who talk to people.

So and so meets so and so from such and such.

And suddenly we're looked at as a cult.

The fact that we weren't yet isolated helped. He still did talks and lectures, then. But drumming, that was something new. It made for an adventure.

We went, all sixty of us, wearing sixty smiles.

And there were so many souls at Venice that the crowd absorbed us.

Still, strange looks. Or was I paranoid? Theodore, he seemed to feel walled in. But Theodore could feel walled in in the desert.

The Leader danced. I loved Him, then.

Still do, of course.

But on that day, to watch Him dance. To watch Him release. The sun bouncing gently upon the horizon. So many girls and boys alight.

'Cause we're all children. He says that, also.

Anybody ever tells you they're a grown-up, you give that motherfucker a second look.

The point is: drumming.

He cursed on that day. Like the lone curse in a PG movie, the one that resonates more so on account of its rarity.

Looking at me, clapping, He said, "Fuck yeah!"

And I laughed so deep right at that moment. Laughed so deep my heart kind of buckled.

Clapping and dancing. Sand crunching up between my toes.

Keep drumming, I kept on telling myself. I don't know why. The words kept bubbling up. I wasn't stoned, nor tripping, nor drunk.

Just, the words kept asserting themselves.

Keep drumming. Keep drumming.

Keep on drumming.

The drums were the sound of the universe entire. The thrum. The momentum. The total depth. Depth in service of depth.

Keep on drumming.

And then I got it. It finally hit me.

Action.

That's the thing we have. Life won't get solved within our heads, much less our aching hearts.

I got it on all fours, while scrubbing the tiles – I really did.

But on that day-night, I got it hard.

The drumming. Perfect. An illustration penned in reality's gushing nectar.

Keep on drumming.

Twenty-Three

Last Day – 9:19AM

And now we're in a situation involving knives.

The kitchen. 'Tween the island and the drawers, facing the former. We're so close that I feel like His arm's around me, even though He has both hands on the island.

Nine steak knives. Glistening. One of them wears the two overhead bulbs like glaring eyes.

This I didn't know about. It raises the stakes (steaks? puns even when your minutes are draining). I expected pills, perhaps, and thought He was to be taken metaphorically when speaking of blood.

"You don't have to say it," He says, "I know what you're thinking. Steak knives are all they had left. A little too Alfred Hitchcock for my taste, but what do you expect at the supermarket, right?"

I release a breathy laugh. Strange considering that I find nothing funny about this.

Last night, before I slipped out, He slipped out. I heard Him go. I was pretty certain that no one else did. That's the bond. That's the second's role.

However, unlike a good assistant, I had no knowledge of where He went till now.

Although when I heard that engine grind on, I must admit that I felt a little hopef--

"Not bad for midnight shopping," I say, making sure again not to pause for long.

My breath, however, is making that hard. All morning, it's been at me like a son of a bitch. Heart of mine, too: a boiling toad.

"My thoughts exactly," He says to me, and do you see what He did right there? Built me up and broke me down in one swift statement. Built me up 'cause He agreed, broke me down 'cause He claims to have beaten me to the thought.

This guy, I'd follow into hell. Existent or otherwise.

Twenty-Four

From KNOWING NARCISSUS by Sheila Powell (pg. 289):

Unfortunately, there is no standard form of measurement to know whether or not you're in an encounter with a narcissist. However, if all of my experience and research has produced anything of value in this regard, it's what I like to call the "ambient bend."

This is a feeling that all of us have sometimes. It's important to know the difference between when this feeling is actually occurring and when we're imagining it. I would regret it if any reader misused this concept to label someone a narcissist who is not.

That said, the "ambient bend" is when you get a feeling from another person that, despite everything being fine and even cordial on the surface, something is really wrong. More specifically, the wrongness seems to relate to how that person feels about you.

One classic archetype who creates this haunting sensation is what we'll call The Helper. The Helper is here to rescue you. Never mind the fact that you were doing okay, or better, before The Helper arrived; The Helper will promise to make your life better than it ever was before.

The Helper uses the same principles that advertisers use. He or she makes you feel bad about yourself, then promises to be the source of making you feel better. He or she will tell you that you're overweight, then promise to go to the gym with you every day and night. This is, essentially, a person who will slap you with one hand and stroke you with the other.

Oftentimes, when The Helper emerges, so does the "ambient bend." Things seem wrong. However, we often blame ourselves for this feeling, for surely the supposed Helper only has the very best of intentions. This pattern of behavior is not uncommon in overbearing employers, military chieftains, and even the leaders of religious organizations (alternative and otherwise).

Twenty-Five

Last Day – 9:20AM

From His pocket, He produces a piece of bread. Peanut butter and jelly slashed about its surface. One piece; He gobbles it down like a cookie. My salivary glands lurch forward.

As He chews, gently, He explains: "Now, everybody of course will get one for themselves. I expect reluctance there; they might want assistance."

"I understand."

"No, I want to be clear: We give no assistance. Each person must act on their own."

Twenty-Six

Edgar Pike's Journal

January, 2008

My mother would say to me, "Edgar: Be clear."

Her mind was very itchy. Almost all the time. Sometimes she was relaxed, often in the car. Car rides north to the relatives on the weekends. Good trees at our sides and a nice glide in the vehicle. I can feel it. It makes my penis tender.

Obviously, though, the car was what put her at ease. All the motion and stimulus. Wasn't real ease, not on her inside. NEVER! Oh, to think of her. I have a love; it's there. But there was always "Be Clear, Edgar."

I'd walk into the kitchen and find her with a friend. The friend would ask how I was doing in school. I'd ramble some bit, going on about English and then Math and then Science. But my mother's agitation would come at me. She'd say, "Lots of topics, Edgar! How about taking them one at a time? Like you do during the day, at school?"

It made sense. I liked it. It made me straighten up. Even, consistent, fine. Get in there deep. FINE!

But looking back, I can recall the friends seeming uptight when they heard her talk to me that way.

* * *

If you take steadiness and fineness to their outermost extremes, you're left with a very clean hum.

This Is What I'm Getting At!

It needn't be more than that. More than that defeats the purpose. It's the still center within us all. You get there, you see it, and you see we're all the same. We're all ONE. Everybody, even the most mentally diseased member of the community, has that in there somewhere.

You get there: *You're CLEAN. You can live there, too. It's intelligent.*

Twenty-Seven

Last Day – 9:21AM

Now our eyes make contact. And I'm reasonably certain that my breath's making contact with His face.

"Okay," I say.

"It has to be that way, Matthew. Otherwise we have murderers in this house. That's not the way to do this. So we be systematic. Wrists and throats all across the board. I have a preference for throats 'cause I think that goes faster. Plus there's none of that vertical-horizontal confusion."

I give Him a look, hoping briefly that I don't have to explain that I'm confused.

I don't.

"Come here. Give me your hand."

He's not asking. He's got my forearm. Other hand, He picks up one of the knives. Briefly, I see myself as a failed test experiment. The others coming in from breakfast, viewing my corpse.

"What's the matter?" He asks me. "You okay?"

"Okay," at this moment, reminds me of "existentialism." Who can say?

Nevertheless, I nod my head. Three times/neck creaking.

"I'm not gonna hurt you. You trust me?"

"Yes, always."

It's He who laughs now, His own breath healthy and forceful. As He goes on speaking, He mimes with the knife, using it as a prop:

"You go vertical, see? Along the veins. That way you're releasing more blood all at once. You go horizontal, all of that gets lost. They always get it wrong on TV. And you should go deep, also..."

He draws the knife up toward my inner elbow. Intimacy like this, you only find in warfare.

"Really get in there. I don't want people laying around dying. They have to go just like *that*."

He drops the knife onto its siblings.

Twenty-Eight

Last Day – 9:23AM

It's the living room, now. Darker and theoretically more comfortable. Still, they "eat" outside, even though the food is surely gone.

He sits on the footrest of a plush armchair. Opposite Him, on the couch, is me. A diagonal line between us.

In His hands, crisp and upright, is a sheet of printer paper. His eyes are fixed upon it, catching the mildest hint of its whiteness.

He lowers the paper, considers addressing me. His lips change. He thinks better of it, keeps on reading.

I'm not good. Sitting is not my thing. I'd like to stand and run and scream.

"You and me I'd like to go last," He says.

He's speaking now of the order, which is a topic of importance.

I nod. I don't like this topic. I just hope it goes fast, like He said. One after another, to the point where the order doesn't stand out. Dizziness. Hot blood rushing. Just get out of here.

"Okay," I say.

"I think that goes without saying, no? They probably sort of expect it."

I clasp my hands together, only these aren't hands. Where's the warmth? The confidence that I can bend my fingers?

I think, then, of Jolie, as her juice is on my fingertips from before.

"Jolie," He says, "I'm sure you're concerned about. She'll go right before you. So that's three of us, which leaves six."

Is that clairvoyance? The collective unconscious? The thought of her arose within my mind right when He said her name.

That's my guy. And He's got me covered. I *was* concerned about her. Not right then, but still.

Hanging near His knees is the paper, the print on its surface concealed from me.

"How do you reckon we should do it?"

Apparently the paper holds no plan. Only the schedule, most likely.

I open my mouth despite its lack of a ready reply.

"Alphabetical, I thought of already. But I'd rather not go that way."

"Right," I say. Safe ground, agreeing. "'Cause then we'd have to be alphabetical, too."

"Not just that, but I think it'll bring too much of a 'grade school' feel. We need something more in contact with the spiritual."

"Yeah, uh..." I shake my head. "No, that's no good."

"What is it?"

"No, I was gonna say size-place-order, but that's grade school, too."

"It's gotta be something that seems second nature," He says, the paper flapping in His hand, "otherwise we'll start getting too much input. This is why we left the corporate world. Right? Bunch of nonsense."

"Yeah," I say, "not to mention the physical world."

"Exactly," He says, and before I know it He's standing.

Twenty-Nine

Last Day – 9:26AM

We're looking out through the patio window, at the others.

"Can I ask a favor of you, Matthew?" He asks.

"Of course." I get the sense that the conversation about the order has been postponed. He will act aloof to the point where I'll expect it to never come up again, and then, right when I least expect it, He'll bring it up like we were just talking about it.

"Explain to the others. About the knives. It should come from you. Tell them not to worry, that we'll make certain they all go gracefully."

Inwardly, I sift around for a frame of reference, another task that's the equal of this one. Was telling all the members to hang in there after little Victor's death the same? Hopefully not, given my low rate of return.

"Will you do that for me?" He asks.

I'll try, that much I know.

But I assure Him that I'll succeed.

Thirty

Edgar Pike's Journal

November, 2007

To be a leader, one has to take a philosophical approach. To be a leader without philosophy is akin to being a sun without a galaxy. In other professions, philosophy is optional. You can drive a bus, or be a lawyer, or even a doctor or an artist, without philosophy (although it's unlikely to go without it in the latter parts of that list). You cannot lead without philosophy. You cannot lead, in other words, and be mindless. This is not to say that you must give your followers a philosophy -- even though in my case it is essential -- but that you must have A Philosophy Of Leadership.

I am getting toward a point where I am not only of a clear philosophy, but where that philosophy is intersecting quite well with my behavior. There must be no bumps, however! Lumps, neither. I must be smooth. Seamless. I must aspire to a kind of white-fire conduct, where it's all consistent to the point of being utterly confidence-inspiring.

So today, when Matthew came to me and asked (such a sweet boy) if I ever have doubts, I must admit to being prideful in both the rapidness and content of my reply:

"Yes," I said. "I have only doubts. Doubts are openness. Doubts keep you alive. A man without doubts, you should run away from."

I was able to do this without ever having pondered the topic before. This indicates a clean link between my brain and mouth. The boy was impressed, too. So much so that he failed to see the paradox: that a man who always doubts has no doubt about the allure of doubting. But that's a topic for another day.

Thirty-One

Last Day – 9:27AM

Out back, the sun lands on me with all the subtlety of a building falling over.

Everyone's lounging. The fruit, as predicted, is gone. The sun they seem to like better than I do.

"I miss her," I hear Beth say to Jolie. "And I think about her a lot. More and more. We were best friends."

I try to catch Jolie's face, get a message as to what the pair's content is. But Jolie's wrapped up in what Beth's saying. I've learned from The Leader to be a guessing man, though, and my best guess is that Beth's talking about her mom.

Thirty-Two

From THE MODERN GLOBE (*10/25/11*):

TV fans know Beth McKay (44) from the 90s soap series “At Odds,” in which she starred as the anguished, lonely wife of a billionaire captain of industry. Ms. McKay said in 1998: “I know the show’s an entertainment vehicle, but I also think it does make a statement. It makes a statement about how the material things in our lives aren’t the most important, and how we sometimes get caught up in that, but what really matters is what’s inside the heart.”

Given the actress’s idealism, it may not come as a great surprise that she is among the nine cult followers whom the press is calling “The Missing Nine.” These people vanished at the start of this month, having followed Mr. Edgar Pike (58) of Santa Barbara to an unknown location.

At least four dozen other followers elected not to go on this mission, which many of them are vocal in believing will culminate in the deaths of The Missing Nine, either at their own hands or the hands of their leader.

TMG spoke with Elisabeth McKay, Beth’s mother:

“My daughter is a genius. Always has been. We knew from a very young age that she was talented. But anybody who knows a genius knows that that doesn’t save you. The only thing that can save her now is common sense. The same intelligence that the rest of us have. If she’s able to see inside of herself and find it.”

Thirty-Three

Last Day – 9:28AM

Not a good tangent to slip into. Seeing/guessing this makes me proceed into my task:

“Guys,” I say. “I have something to share with all of you.”

I try to sound like He does whenever I can. Give the words a little sculpting. And in the ways of Him, I position myself as close as I can to the others’ center.

“It’s about tonight.”

“Everthing we do today is about tonight, isn’t it?” This is Michael speaking. He’s like that. You say, “sky,” and he’ll come back with “ground.”

Thirty-Four

Email sent from Michael Graves to his coworkers (5/11/08):

Fellow slaves,

I know that while I've sat in my cell – sorry, I mean "cubicle" – I was supposed to be thinking all kinds of passionate thoughts about our latest exciting new containers, and how our sealing effectiveness was improving due to data from Japan or some such fucking bullshit.

What I was thinking, and what I want you to know, was a lot of thoughts about dignity. It seems that nobody spends time on that concept much anymore.

Dignity is what makes us people. A dog doesn't have dignity. A dog shits on the ground. A human can or cannot have dignity. It's up to (a) us and (b) the people around us, whose energy influences us.

Me, I want to have dignity. You guys don't want me to, though. You talk to me like I'm vibrating at a low frequency. Every day, driving home, for two years now, I've had anger. I'll yell at the other cars, but I'm really yelling at you.

Sorry for any past confusion. Now I'm addressing you directly: You are weak. You are mediocre. You haven't taken more than a passing glance at reality. You certainly never even flexed an eyeball toward me.

I don't wish anything bad upon you, but only because there's so much of it already there.

Your friend,

Michael (aka Slave who Woke Up)

Thirty-Five

Last Day – 9:29AM

"Yes, Michael, but more specifically, it's about our mode of...exit."

I now have their attention.

"I know in the past, The Leader has spoken of the possibility of us taking something with our dinner. But I've communicated with him, and he has decided that we are to do it with knives instead."

Paul says, "Slit our wrists," in a way that doesn't quite get around to being a question.

"Yes. Or the throat, if you prefer."

And here I can't get a read on them. I then hear myself rushing, and with each word I say, I feel like I'm sounding more and more full of shit:

"Now, The Leader wanted me to assure all of you that the act of...that it will all be dignified and graceful, and that there is nothing to worry about. Does anyone have any questions?"

This is why I'm not Him. Him? They would be dancing right now.

But no one's gaze is coming near mine. Not even Jolie's.

"All right, then," I say, the embodiment of failure. "Group Talk Session starts in fifteen. I'll see all of you there."

Needing Jolie like a swimmer needs the shore, I go in her direction. And she in mine.

Then past me.

She slips her way, frowning, back into the door I came out of.

Thirty-Six

Last Day – 9:44AM

And now an emergency has graced our world.

'Cause Group Talk Session starts in one, and Jolie is in the goddamn bathroom. Not our bathroom, the hallway bathroom.

And as if my heart's not contorting enough, The Leader's in His own room, some thirty feet away. I don't know what He's doing in there, but I hear a drawer opening and closing, and something like metal clanging atop wood.

He sees us, we're fucked. He may not believe in time, but He hates lateness.

I tap the door with my knuckle, much preferring to knock. Much preferring, in fact, to split the fucking thing open with my fist.

"Jolie?" A hiss.

She's fast to answer, which shows some commitment: "What?"

But she's also crying, which sets off my alarms.

"Baby..." An impersonation of a calm, caring man. "What're you doing in there?"

"What does it sound like?"

That question too loud. My head spins to the left. His doorway. Open. Light flowing from it. Not Him, though.

"Open the door," I say. Better to be in there than out here.

"No."

My stomach: taking punches from inside.

"Come on, Jolie. Please."

And – then – strange – words: "Can't do this anymore."

A wildfire lights up my ears. If I could fuse my eyes to His doorway, I would. He's deep in there, though, it seems. More clanging about.

But then I hear drawers closing. Finishing sounds.

"Jolie: quiet. What're you talking about?"

"You don't just switch things around." Sounding hurt. "It's the last day."

"Babe, you gotta -- Let me in. Come on."

"Knives?!" The word embedded with tears. "Is he fucking serious?"

My peripheral vision draws in a storm cloud. I turn.

It's Him.

Staring.

My skeleton jumps before the rest of me.

"We're starting the session now," He says, words so dry they could crumble.

"Be right there," I say, acting normal.

Only this right here is far from normal. He doesn't wait, and I don't make Him.

And Jolie: She certainly would never make me make Him.

Nodding, He walks away, yet even when He's gone, I still feel like He's watching.

"Damn it." This to myself.

“Jolie. We have to go. The session’s starting.”

This to her.

Thirty-Seven

Last Day – 9:55AM: GROUP TALK SESSION

I get her, and I ignore the tears on her cheeks when she comes out, a fact for which I hate myself.

Though I hate myself more for being late, and the way my throat feels, I'll be shocked the next time I swallow.

When we go into the living room, they're all there, cross-legged on the hardwood floor. He sees us come in, though not with His eyes. It makes Him happy, our appearance, though He's not about to actually look.

And in any event, Beth is speaking:

"It was the tabloids that really did it. I know they're silly, and that I shouldn't have cared. But I did. I would just buy them every day and root through them for any mention of me. Some days, it was like a game. Like, before I would open one up, I'd try to guess, *What awful thing are they saying about me now*?"

Beth, of course, is something of a celebrity. One of those shows where all the rooms are missing a front wall, and none of the lamps ever need to be turned on.

Jolie is maiming me as we walk, wiping the corners of her eyes.

"I didn't know how *not* to care," Beth says. "I didn't know how to ignore it. How do you ignore cruelty, when it's smiling right in your face like that?"

She, too, tries to talk like Him sometimes. And like me, she tends to fall short.

"Well, in this case, Beth, you were seeking it out by purchasing that nonsense." The Leader's tone is even; His content, scolding.

"You're right. I was. I'm lucky I had my mom through it all, though. She kept me sane."

We find our seats amongst them on the floor.

"Um. Anyhow," Beth throws some of her hair back over one shoulder. "All that said, I'm so happy to be sharing tonight with all of you. This is long overdue for me."

Beth looks down into her lap, her head like an upper lip descending.

Now Paul: "Can I say something?"

The Leader says, "Yes."

Paul looks at Beth, who senses as much and looks back up.

"Thanks for sharing, Beth. You are so strong, and it inspires me to be strong."

"Thank you," she says, and I hear that it comes from her chest.

The Leader, no doubt preferring less banality, finally regards our presence. My torso collapses when I see His smile.

"My angels," He says. "You made it."

"Sorry to be late," I say.

But not Jolie, who's without regret.

"No!" The Leader's reply is blaring. "Not a problem. We were just going around the circle and sharing whatever has been coming up for us on this beautiful morning. And perhaps one of you should be next. It looks like you both have something on your minds."

I do my best to meet Jolie's eyes, but like on the patio, they're not available. It's obvious, or should be, that she's the one with the issue. But like outside, I'm the one absorbing the heat.

I say to The Leader, "Well..."

And then get rescued--

Jolie says, "Yes, actually. There is something."

The Leader's eyes go aglow. "We'd be delighted to hear it," He says, and I think He might mean it.

Me? My torso's retying its knots.

She says, "Matthew told us about the knives, and to be honest..."

Him: "Honesty. A noble attribute indeed."

She tries to smile, but it's like the muscles in her face weren't built for it. "Uh, I don't think this is for me."

* * *

We stood there, in the rain.

We stood there, the nine of us.

We stood there, as He wept.

We stood there, watching the others all go.

We stood there, and said we'd be the ones.

We stood there, and made a sacred promise.

We stood there, and told Him that

Unlike Them

We would never, ever, ever leave Him alone.

Thirty-Eight

Last Day – 9:57AM

"What my dear?" The Leader asks, and I'd like very much to go over and hug Him.

"I can't do it. I mean, the blood. And the pain. It's not--"

"Let me ask you something." His words lean, like flattened-out lightning. "Do you think that it will be any more painful than what your father has done to you?"

Now the room goes cold entirely.

Beth and her mother, that's one topic.

Jolie and her father...

"That's different," she says.

"How?" He wants to know.

"Well, I mean, I've never tried it before, but I would imagine that slitting your wrists would be pretty painful."

"Painful, like how?"

"Physically."

"And if there's one thing about the physical world that I've taught you, what is that?"

"Well..." Chiseling coldness. "...that it doesn't exist?"

"Exactly. Which means--?"

"That physical pain doesn't exist."

"Correct. And now, think back to your father."

"I don't want to."

"This'll only be for a minute."

Jolie takes a breath.

"Think of the pain that he has inflicted upon you. The deep emotional scars that he has dug into your body. The wretchedness of it all. Years of scars crusted upon scars, crusted upon *other* scars. They aren't physical; they aren't surface-like; they're deeper than that. They cut into your *heart*, not just your veins. You feel that, don't you?"

And she says, "Yes."

"And so, will you not be able to endure a mere moment of physical pain? Especially if it allows you to travel to eternity with the ones whom you love the most?"

Quietness like this, we may as well have left the planet already.

"I think I can," she goes.

"I know you can." And His voice has changed, indicating a rattling spike of pleasure. "You've come so far, my dear. In mere hours, you will release all the suffering in your heart for good. And no one will be able to hurt you anymore. I promise."

And now she cries. But not like in the bathroom.

"I would love that so much," she says to Him.

A gesture from The Leader, now.

We are to go to her, and hug her close.

Soon Jolie is surrounded, then in a latticework of arms. I find myself doing something odd, however.

I don't join.

I watch.

This only happens for a moment.

The Observer.

But then I go. We all hold her, minus Him.
And Beth says, “Sweet Jolie.”
We sway.
And Jolie cries, then sighs, then laughs.
A laugh of ecstasy from deep inside.

Thirty-Nine

From a C-ABC Interview with Chester and Monica True (11/4/11):

C-ABC: Tell us about your daughter, Jolie...

(Pause.)

C-ABC: Her name is French for "pretty," is it not?

CT: It is.

MT: Yes, it is. And she is that.

C-ABC: We can only imagine how much you must miss her at this hour.

(Pause.)

CT: Oh, we do. We do. Very much. More than words... More than we're able to be articulate about.

MT: We hope she can hear this, though.

CT: Yes.

MT: We hope that, Jolie... You can give life another chance.

CT: She was a talented girl.

C-ABC: An acumen for painting, music...

CT: Oh, yes sir. Painting, music. A very light spirit. She shined a light. And I can see how a man like...their commander, or whatever they call him...I can see how a man like that would want to be around her.

MT: 'Cause she's good. She's really good.

CT: Yes sir. That is correct.

MT: She's the type of person who will smile at you if she thinks you've having a bad day. She sees the upside of things.

CT: Not this...garbage that's being fed to her.

C-ABC: "Garbage," you call it.

CT: Oh, yes sir. Bunch of dangerous ideas. Doesn't help nobody but him.

Forty

From a C-ABC interview with Allison Roth (*11/6/11*):

C-ABC: And you've also been quite controversial in your statements about Jolie True...

AR: Only controversial to her family.

C-ABC: How is that?

AR: I've repeated what Jolie True told me.

C-ABC: Which is what?

AR: Which is that there was molestation in her home.

C-ABC: Despite the risk of a defamation lawsuit.

AR: They've talked about that, but I've claimed no knowledge of the facts, only what Jolie True told me: From a very young age, there was abuse in the home. If you want to call me in to talk about this lifestyle, then that's part of it. What he did to me was not new to us. Many of us had been touched before in our lives.

C-ABC: And you feel that when it comes to Ms. True in particular, this led to what many are expecting to be a suicidal outcome?

AR: Yes.

(Pause.)

AR: It's not normal when a girl behaves as she did. Very sweet. She never got in any fights. There were no problems. But when a young lady like her offers to...perform oral sex on you if you're having a bad day...

C-ABC: She made this offer to you?

AR: She was promiscuous. Eventually, she had a boyfriend, and then the dirty mouth stuff ended. But it wasn't unusual for her or many of the girls – and women – there to be sexually on display as a way of feeling good about themselves and keeping the leader happy. This was every day.

Forty-One

Last Day – Matthew Thinking Back

After the rains were gone, He came to me. Said something that He'd never said before. Perhaps He'd said it to Jed, when Jed was second in charge, but Jed, the selfish fuck, wouldn't have believed Him anyway.

But to me, He said He loved me.

And that was important. And it made me cry.

For my father never told me that. Nor my mom.

And Jolie had told me, but after she had, she'd said the saddest thing:

"But I have to say I'm not sure if I believe in love. I'm not saying that to hurt you, Matthew. I'm saying that because of..."

Tears.

"...my dad. What he did. It was too much. It was every day. And over and over. And he liked it too much. And the way he smiled.

"He broke my heart too many times.

"But whatever of my heart is left, I give to you."

And I took that from her, I did – but it wasn't enough.

Because I loved – love – her with colossal might.

And fuck her father, yes, but fuck her, too, a little bit. (Apologies for the word, given what he did.)

The Leader, though, what He said was pure. 'Cause not only did He offer love, but He told me that He'd never, ever done so. Not in this way.

Not at this depth.

We held each other.

Years before, I would have deemed that strange. It wasn't sexual, but it was still two men. We held each other, though, and we dozed off after a while.

And in between my strands of sleep, when I woke and saw Him there, I felt so perfect.

A nectar drip inside.

Warmth like the sun can't even imagine.

Forty-Two

Edgar Pike's Journal

July, 2009

I could go down on Matthew. I've no interest in penises, generally. But he has such a nectarine sweetness, that boy. Jed, too, but Jed is older. I could service Matthew, and be the slave, and be free in being the slave.

Forty-Three

Last Day – 11:00AM: CHORES

Finally, now, I've got Jolie.

Chores in the library (or at least it was once). We're cleaning the large bay windows, their heat pressing through the paper towels in our hands, their light making all the spray sparkle when it lands.

Cathleen's got the empty bookshelves, but I'm in the light with Jolie.

She's humming now. No more tears.

I look at her, closely. That face of perfection. "You okay?" I ask.

"Yeah," she goes.

At which point all my systems cool. My flapping mind comes in for landing.

All is stable. He actually managed to carry her home. Truth told, she hasn't seemed so centered in days.

Off-center, however, is my heart, which starts right away to do its thing again.

Forty-Four

Last Day – 11:04AM

The kitchen's got Susan, Michael, and Paul down on their knees, a bend away from praying as they scrub the floor. Since we wear no shoes, the tiles get oils on them every day. But when the marks are gone, the floor shimmers so hard your feet could buzz.

Their work is fine, by which I mean "superior" rather than "okay." A good, deep effort, defined by rigor and concentration. No errant thoughts get in its way. No distractions brought on by how much money will be gained (none) nor how their mouths will be fed (He's got them covered).

And for a moment, inwardly, I am idle at last...

Until I look out through the window, toward the patio, and see The Leader in conversation with Theodore.

More Theodore. He's loomed too large all day.

With an interest in feeling in control, I ask everyone if they're okay.

"Yes," says Susan. "We're fine."

By which she means "okay."

"Good," I say, but I've disengaged.

I've got to go upstairs and get my phone.

Forty-Five

Last Day – 11:06AM

I think that we all heard me correctly.

This is me, now, walking down the upstairs hallway.

The Leader's locked deep in discussion with Theodore, and since talking to Theodore can get kind of thorny, I'm guessing that I have some time.

Not much (after all, it doesn't exist), but a few minutes.

And that's all I need to see The Leader's nightstand.

My head does everything it can to stop me: The wall paint's swimming. Little dots float inside of/around my eyes.

The door's open, however; that's how much He trusts us.

When I step through it, though, that trust will become a mockery.

But it's just an experiment. It isn't serious. Like this morning with the lawn. It's a whim, me getting pulled by strings.

Would like to see my phone, is all. Just to know where it is, in case Jolie gets scared again. Or Theodore keeps on throwing me looks.

When I'm finally in the room, I feel the whole space bending – curving its white body around me. And it's as though I sense the ticking of some soundless, invisible clock.

I pace. The room bends more. The nightstand comes at me.

My eyes: the doorway.

Empty.

Be silent. This will take a moment.

You're just a boy who wants to see what's in a drawer. You should be no more tense than you would if the target were a cookie jar.

Hand: metal. Arm: pulling. Drawer: creaking.

Slower! Are-you-fucking-crazy?

But of course I am.

But Jolie was crying about those knives. Don't misremember. Those tears flowed real. "Isn't for me," she said, as though there were an actual her, and this were an actual world.

The drawer's now open, and shining color at me are the phones. Batteries? That would take more time. For now, I'm content to let my eyes go to my phone.

Sleek red. Brings car paint to mind. (Do I spy cardboard?)

And apparently my hand's content to go to it, too.

'Cause now it's--

--Eyes/door/empty–

The phone's in my pocket, now. And I'm pacing out of here like the floor's on fire.

Forty-Six

Last Day – 11:08AM

Made it into the bathroom without my bronchial tubes plugging up. Jolie and my bathroom, not the one in the hall. There's a wheeze inside me, though throat or chest is hard to say. Throat would be a relief since my heart's so swelled and busy. Chest would be a relief since it'd mean my throat's okay.

Not that I'll still have either come the dusk.

Here in my hand we have a remnant from the world. An artifact as foreign as a fallen shard of spaceship, yet (admit it) comforting all the same.

Within my head, right now, are choices.

I can reverse my trajectory, as though life was in a DVD player and I was pressing rewind. Get out of here. Back to The Leader's room. Phone in drawer. Drawer closed nice.

Status quo brought back full force.

Or I can depress the black button and see if there's life. Irony here: Dying boy in search of life. If there is life, the odds of me pressing more buttons get real high.

Leader's room or not, I'm still in the tiger's mouth. This door could open right now and I'd get melted. Yet, somewhere within the weeds of my mind, I wonder if the fate that greeted me then would be worse than what awaits me later on.

FUCK.

Did I just think that?

Across my mind's eye slips that rain. That night. Our vow.

Hand. Phone. Finger. Button.

Eyes: Door.

Locked. Silent. Vertical rectangle with a gift for staring.

More inhaling, followed by exhaling (wheezing), followed by...

I run the faucet. Its sound slices nerves. Double-check the door's button lock.

Then another button gets pressed. And we've got life.

Holy shit – no batteries removed. My admiration for the man ascends. Love and trust like nothing back in the world. And yet here I am ripping His guts out.

My prediction of myself deserves no prizes for its accuracy...

I check my voicemail. And I have...

"*Twelve new messages*."

That's too much world for me right now. The info makes like jagged fishnet around my brain. I shut the phone off, pocket it near my hip.

And then the door is bending. And there are knocks.

The knocks precede the bending in real life. The whole of my being gets shredded up.

Breath. Mirror. Reflection. Who?

No time. Straighten the white threads. More knocks--

Whatever leaves your mouth next will have to work--

I open it. It's not Him, which is good.

But it's Theodore, which, as you might expect, is not.

"He wants to see you," he says to me, and like every statement out of Theodore's mouth, it has a way of being menacing and benign and off and on all at once.

We're close right now, he and I. Kissing distance. If his eyes bend downward, he could see my gaping pocket. My bare feet bloodless, I walk right toward him, showing the confidence of a pedestrian who knows the cars will have to get out of his way.

Forty-Seven

From private correspondence from Matthew Barrett to his family (*5/2009*):

This is my last time making any kind of contact.

To Dad, I'll say nothing, 'cause he knows how I feel.

To the rest of you, I'll say that, fine, I loved you, and fine, you're not bad people or my enemies. But all of you are lost. None of you can see what I see. If I even started to use the words we use here, you'd roll your eyes. If I told you what my mind is like, now that I've really seen it, you'd think I was just talking crazy.

I don't want the conversation. I want peace, but that doesn't mean we have to be in touch.

Forty-Eight

Last Day – 11:14AM

We're out back now, The Leader and I, a setting that I could do without, on account of all the space and air, and what the former does to my head and the latter does to my chest.

We're far from the house, also, near to the shed. I've only been inside of it once. My head likes to mutter vague fictions about how it's haunted. How murders once took place inside of it.

The Leader's walking exceeds His talking; in fact, He's been wordless since He asked me to "Come along" with Him. So maybe it's time for the shed and some axe and saw work. Maybe He'll show me the side that those two ladies glimpsed. To say nothing of the infant, Victor Garcia.

I think of Victor as we walk. In a sense, he was this day's trail-blazer: the first of the group to die whilst a member. Only in his case it wasn't voluntary, so my connection is perverse at best and psychotic at worst.

His mother killed him, not The Leader. About the ladies, I'll admit to doubts. About little Victor, though, I will know to my dying breath that He is clean.

Mrs. Garcia was macrobiotic. That's a special diet, a rung beyond veganism. No meat, no dairy, no caffeine, no refined sugar, no white flour. I memorized the goddamn list because she spoke of it so much, but for all her speaking, she didn't know a thing.

(The Leader on veganism and its like: "A noble idea, certainly, to not harm animals. But do you know how many bugs you crush while taking an evening stroll?")

Thing was, Mrs. Garcia, in all her lack-of-wisdom, stopped feeding breast milk to her son. She rejected it 'cause she thought it was like cow's milk, which is of course a major source of dairy. As a substitute, she fed him soy milk. However, breast milk, unlike soy milk, is a key source of vitamins, minerals, enzymes, amino acids, and proteins for an infant.

But little Victor got none of the above. And even when you could see his ribs, his mom's eyes remained fairly sturdy.

A lunatic convincing herself that she was sane.

Not one of us was convinced, however, and mind you, we numbered dozens at the time. The Leader Himself was at the market when Victor died.

To say what the house was like at that time would be indecent.

From day one, lots of us had shaken our heads at the baby's presence. Not because we feared for his life (that never crossed a single mind), but because the house was free in terms of Eros and chemicals. Bodies were nude a lot. And The Leader's thoughts on drugs were rather liberal (this before He flushed Theodore's Haldol).

I suppose that our energy cast the boy out. He was unwanted by many, got rejected on a particle level.

It doesn't mean we didn't cry. Doesn't mean our throats didn't lock. But again, some memories are best left gathering dust.

And besides, I'm only thinking of Victor 'cause I sense that I'll be next. We're right by the shed now.

He stops. I stop. Cause and effect. Steals a glance at the house to make sure that we're unobserved.

And then, en route to easing my chest, He begins to speak about Theodore:

"Have you spoken with Theodore since you woke?"

"Not really, no."

"He was talking a certain way to me. I didn't care for it. He asked me why our family is so nice-looking."

I slip my hands inside my pockets. My right one touches the phone and I could scream.

"Sometimes we make little jokes about it," I say.

"'Little' I hope is the key word. I take our beauty seriously."

And now His eyes are on and in me. Handsomeness like few will ever know.

"He told me, as if I didn't already know, that journalists were curious regarding our group's physical appearance. It was a strange conversation. I felt a cramp the whole time."

Is this what we're talking about?

"I'm sure," I say, "all of us are thinking new thoughts."

"That much I encourage. This was an affront, though. He was questioning me."

Now I look toward the house for a moment. Think of Theodore inside of it. Jolie, as well. One asking questions, the other fearing knives.

And then there's me. But my words aim to keep the peace: "Well, you have to keep in mind, he hasn't been on his meds since we got here."

Though I'm not quite certain that that was peacekeeping.

"Well," He says, "medication is administered, simply, to stamp out the spirit. To rip the impulses clean out of a person. In my opinion, Theodore has been much more lucid without those potions. Though I must admit, he still can leave me quite unsettled.

"Especially today.

"Can you speak with him? To calm his mind?"

"I'd love to," I say, even though I wouldn't. "But to be honest, I'm not sure if that will do any good."

His face changes: less handsome/more handsome/ equally handsome.

"Why?" He wants to know. "Because of what occurred when you tried to speak with Jolie?"

In a natural reflex, my head tilts downward. The guilt of a boy with his hand in the cookie jar (with his hand on an actual phone). "I'm sorry about that," I say.

Now His eyes have a softness about them. “She was afraid, that’s all. I should’ve prepared you for something like that, but I didn’t. No need to apologize.”

The cool air of a passing moment. We’ve agreed to let it go.

“So,” He says, “I gave Theodore permission to have a little break in his room. Will you go there and speak to him for me?”

Forty-Nine

Edgar Pike's Journal

November, 2009

Gaining power requires nothing. A gorilla can do it -- and by that I mean mentally, not physically. It's primitive. Power?

All you do is sift around for someone's weakness. It can become apparent within moments if you ask the right questions, act warm enough. You get the weakness, you have the power.

I had a friend once who was afraid of bridges. He told me that the first time we spoke. I acted like I forgot. Then four months later, I suggested we have all our lunches in a restaurant beside the Golden Gate Bridge. He sat there cowed the whole time!

Beth hates talking about the TV show. So I never mention it. But you should see the look on her face when I mention other soaps!

Fifty

Last Day – 11:29AM

Theodore's room might as well be my room. My room might as well be any other room. Whiteness, that's the long and short of it.

As for my thoughts, they may as well be The Leader's thoughts, so filled are they with the words He told me to say.

I go fast, not only 'cause I want to run out of here, but 'cause I'm fearful of forgetting what I have to say. And if this goes the same way His last request did...

"Theodore," I whisper, "can I come in for a minute?"

He's on the floor, legs unbent and parallel. He looks equally saddened and overjoyed to see me.

"Sure," he says.

Kid-like, rapidly, I pull up a piece of floor beside him. Try to make this fun. Should have done so with the knives.

"Your name came up in our conversation," I tell him, my tone so chipper I may as well be saying that there are gifts awaiting him beneath the tree.

"Really?" he asks, and he's really asking. "And what was this conversation about?"

He, too, tries to sound like Him.

I, however, not only sound like Him; I'm actually reciting His words:

"We love you, we said," The Leader says through me. "We have a special love for you."

Theodore's eyes melt.

The Leader then uses my mouth to say: "No more special than for any of the others -- but we want you to witness as much beauty as can be seen without being an actual leader."

"How do you mean?" Theodore's eyebrows descend.

Then The Leader, who's not in the room, says to Theodore: "Well, I can't go into it too much right now, as the order of our passing is to remain a secret, but he and I have decided to let you in on something special."

Suspense that could part the walls from the ceiling.

But when I resume speaking, it's actually me speaking: "You are to go right before The Leader. Tonight. Second to last."

"He said that?"

"Yes."

"*I* go second-to-last? Not you?"

"We decided that it's only fair. We haven't figured out the rest, but after the first five depart, it will be me and Jolie together, followed by you, and then he will be the final one."

Theodore glances up at the ceiling, as if expecting to spy a holy entity. Upon returning to Earth (such as he can), he says, "I hope it doesn't discomfort you, Matthew."

"Why would it?" I furnish up a smile. "It was partially my idea."

“Well, you know in recent years I’ve had thoughts of leadership. And perhaps we spoke less after Jed left and you were promoted.”

That’s it for me. I’m out of here. Not because what he says threatens me; after all, he’s as fit for leadership as Fredo Corleone.

I rise because I’ve closed the deal. I run my palms across my pant legs, relieving them of various specks and bits. “Maybe,” I say, sliding a lie into the chamber, “but regardless, Theodore: I think only good things about you.”

Theodore’s eyes have stopped melting now...as they are entirely melted. He hides them with his hand, turning it into a V-lipped visor.

“There were smiles on our faces,” I say, taking advantage of his emotions, “as we discussed it. Only don’t make any mention of it beforehand, though; act surprised. We don’t want any drama in this house.”

This time, unlike on the patio, I am coolness personified. I have him. So much so that I don’t even have to hang ‘round for a verbal confirmation.

By the time I leave, he’s become less man than puddle.

Fifty-One

Last Day – 11:20AM

But that's not what The Leader said out back.

What I said was close, and I quoted Him as much as possible, but at the last moment, I changed it up a little.

'Cause you see, The Leader, for reasons best known to Himself--

Said that He wanted Theodore to go *third* to last. Theodore-Me-Leader.

Which leaves Jolie where?

I asked The Leader that very question before going up to see Theodore, working my words in amidst an assault of wheezes.

By way of an answer, He said, "That breath must be agitating for you. What can I do to calm you down?"

Quite hot inside, I repeated myself: "Where does Jolie go in the order?"

The Leader actually looked down at the grass. As though He had yet to consider that part.

As though His fucking objective was to tear me down.

"Naturally," He said, "your thoughts would be with her."

Since He was looking downward, I robbed a moment to check my pulse. My fingers went to my neck, got used like a punching bag by my veins. He saw me do it, looked up before I stopped.

His frown nearly poked my bladder into pissing.

"I'll devote some more thought to your girlfriend," He said. "We'll discuss it after lunch."

My girlfriend? Who's that?

He'd never called her that before. "Love" and "soul mate" and "second heart," yes, but never "girlfriend."

As I watched Him go, I thought again of the shed. How would it have gone if we were actually in there?

Might I have been the one with the axe and saw?

Fifty-Two

Last Day – 11:24AM

Is this a test? I asked myself in the backyard.

One final exercise to refine my gush? Make me feel the innermost nuances of reality?

Make me watch my "girlfriend," who's afraid of knives, die, both of us stripped clean of the comfort that I'll go next?

I looked at the back of that hairless head. His exit a way of telling me He was done with me. I'd received my orders, and I was to comply with wind-up toy predictability.

Who was I looking at, was the question.

A He or a he?

Was I in the hands of a mighty force, or a petty ex-computer salesman?

* * *

'Cause that's what He did, see. Before He wore white.

Sold computers. Was an affiliate for a second-rate company, had His own website and PayPal account.

Thoughts of taxation and shipping in His mind.

Beer and TV in the evenings. Soap operas like the one He rescued Beth from.

Fifty-Three

Last Day – 11:32AM

And as I went to Theodore's door, I felt something toward Him I had never felt. I'm reluctant to use the actual word.

But after I *exit* Theodore's door, having delivered the wrong news, effectively introducing fly to ointment, I have another feeling, and this one I'll share.

For this one I am not ashamed of.

I close Theodore's door. Check my pocket. Still, the phone.

And inside me, briefly: Joy!

Fifty-Four

Edgar Pike's Journal

July, 2009

The great revelation of college is how stupid everyone is. During the build-up before college, one fears the competition. Fears getting out there and into the big leagues. The big leagues, when you reach them, are small and flawed. Everywhere, it's like this.

I wasn't at all experienced in the ways of blackmail when I met Drew. I sold computers; kept it straight and clean. Only Drew insisted on referring to his money. Ran several companies. Kept making purchases. And then he wished to give me a present...

It'll sound insincere, but I knew from Drew's first mentions of "his" money that it was actually "my" money. I knew it would flow my way, and that something fortuitous and BIG would have to happen to make that happen.

I feel so bad for Drew, but he's so wealthy. I'm sure he's worried sick, but he needn't worry. I got what I wanted. $900,000 in exchange for agreeing to hide the photo of him and the small boy. It was on the hard drive of the computer that he wished so badly to give me. I found it quite easily, even though he'd tried to delete it – and then to delete the deletion. I knew, straight and clear, that when he insisted on gifting me that machine, there was something polluted about it. Like he wanted it away from his house. He should've thrown it from a bridge!

The only evidence now remaining is this entry. I burned the cursed computer; didn't he realize that my possession of that image was criminal, also? (Less so for me than for him, yet still not something you want to keep around the house.) The deal was made by phone and the transaction in cash. When I took the cash, I thought about how stupid this man was. You want to get rid of something; you get rid of it. Don't leave it hanging around: stomp it, crush it, destroy it!

But I knew: my third eye. The cash had to be mine. And the plan had no glitches or tight spots in it at all.

Fifty-Five

Last Day – 11:33AM

I must call Jed.

Fifty-Six

Last Day – 11:34AM

But let's not get carried away.

Jed, I hate. His cigarettes and facial expressions. Trying to revive James Dean. He's around, the bullshit meter spikes.

Theodore may eye me with thoughts of power, but Theodore is dreaming. Me, when I eyed Jed with those thoughts, I was firmly in reality.

'Cause I was His best friend, and everyone knew it.

The ease between The Leader and I was plainer than day. Than Jane.

And when Jed went like the traitor he is, guess who got promoted?

Fifty-Seven

Last Day – 11:35AM

But I call Jed. Don't even have to check the messages. All twelve are from him or my head's made of rocks. Bricks, maybe – I'll grant that – but not rocks, far as I know.

The chores, by now, should be relaxing. It's getting near enough to Downtime, which goes from twelve to one. Which means we can do whatever we want (short, of course, of what I'm doing).

Same routine as before, in seamless facsimile:

Door locked. Faucet on. Phone out.

Only this time one added step:

Speed. Dial.

And if I thought the world was in my ear before, then Jed shows me how wrong I was. 'Cause Jed is world and solar system and galaxy.

Jed is the universe, screaming with relief. Probably some pride as well, since he's getting a call from the place the whole media and half the police are looking for:

"Matthew! Oh, thank God!"

He's bald, he's earnest, but he's got that slant in his voice, still.

This is Jed.

No police around him, that I know. His record's far too long for that.

"Don't be loud," I tell him. "Don't be loud."

"Are there people with you? There's something I have to s--"

"I'm in the bathroom. There's not much time. I have no charger."

"Did you get my messages? I left like twenty."

Urgent: "I didn't listen. There's no time for anything. This is the last day."

This news doesn't land the way I'd thought. His momentum stays intact like he knew it or expected it or is onto something else--

"Are you – wheezing?"

And suddenly, you know, I feel so sad. The room tilts and the toilet comes up to accommodate my rear. Lid is up, so I'm drooping down. Comical in a way that fails to arrive at funny.

Fifty-Eight

Edgar Pike's Journal
March, 2008

I don't like the word that talks about air expelling from the buttocks. I don't like it and I hope others don't like it, although I sense that everybody might. When I was born, and until the late 1980s or early 1990s, it was something in the direction of a curse word. Not quite like "fuck," which I don't mind, generally, but lower in a way. More disgusting and pitiful. Yet everyone says it. Children on sitcoms! From their little mouths!

I do confess to liking the feeling. In that regard I'm in the mainstream. RASP! Sometimes on my palm, then palm to face. Do we all do this?

It's important, these things. To know what reality is really like. Otherwise, it's a lie layer cake that just gets higher and higher.

Every day, I see my feces in the toilet. Every day, chunks on lines of floss. Thoughts about killing somebody who angers me. Dick getting hard when a fourteen-year-old walks by. Okay? Doesn't mean I'll kill, nor molest.

But to not say these things -- where's that leave us?

Fifty-Nine

Last Day – 11:37AM

Then I cry. If he can hear the wheezing, he can hear this, too.

"I'm not feeling good," I say, although it does feel good to tell someone that. "I don't know what to do. He has high expectations."

"Matthew, listen to me: You don't want this. Okay? You have to listen to me."

"Lower your voice, please. Lower your voice."

Is it possible that he's being louder than me?

My nose is snotty. I snort it back gently and silently: an infant.

"I knew you. We all knew you. I remember how you talked about life."

And those are certainly words I can do without. The bathroom gets cold enough to make me picture Pluto. I've split so far from the program, I may as well be in outer space. This bathroom an outpost, surrounded by dark and stars.

"I know," I say. "I remember, too."

Eyes on the door, but weak, now. Droopy, a little. The tears. My sinuses. The beating dished out from my chest: Non. Stop.

"Matthew, we're prepared to intervene. I can bring a van. Everybody but him is welcome to come."

And then, crisp and colorful, I have a head full of kings. Kings in robes, hundreds of years ago, toasting wine pooled in silver goblets.

Did those kings not have treachery within their castles?

Were there not always others who wished to overthrow them?

Often – admit it – seconds in command?

I have to really ask myself what this is about, 'cause I'm swimming in waters where the sharks roam thick. And if it's about power, then I'm a pathetic sell-out.

Even worse, it could be about the lack of food in my body.

Blood sugar low and delusions high.

The Leader once asked me, in the old house, what it's called when you think you've seen your dead grandma still alive.

I shrugged and smiled.

"Delusions of Grandma," He said, and we both laughed.

I could laugh now, too, if there wasn't Jed to hear it.

I say to Jed, precise and fast: "He expects a lot from us. We have no time."

And either Jed starts multiplying or he starts repeating himself: "You have time. You have time. You have time. You're a young man. You could have years if you want."

My teeth and my lip, seeing which will crack first.

"And you do want them," he says. "You do want them. If you can listen to him, you can listen to me."

And that was always the problem with fucking Jed. Put power anywhere near the guy's head, and it'll ignite till the whole universe gets charred.

"I have to go," I say. "I can't be talking."

"Matthew!" He's loud. If anyone is out in the room, they most certainly think I've got Jed in here. "Hear me now! You called because you wanted help. That is inside of you. *You called me back because you wanted help*."

"Have to go," I say (truth). "You're a very, very nice man, Jed." (lie)

"And so are you. So are you. You belong in this world. You don't belong with him. Do I have to mention all the plans you had? You were gonna do good things on this planet, Matthew."

If what happens now isn't hyperventilation, then I hope I never know what the real thing feels like. Only, come on: Did I ever have plans? We were in it for the gush, not for hard results. A guy like Jed was supposed to understand that.

"Yeah, well," I say, so weak I could vanish, "the planet's looking pretty dark, Jed."

"Which is why we need y--"

"Please don't call me anymore."

"Listen to the voicemails!"

I breathe out a magic carpet of breath. Upon it ride the words "So long, Jed."

"No, wait, Matthew--!"

Black button again.

Turn off the world.

Then the faucet, as well. Wanting nothing from out there to be in here.

* * *

The last time I saw Jed, we were in me and Jolie's room in the old house. Jolie was in the bathroom, taking a bath. She'd been up all night crying about Victor's passing. But after the detectives came, she switched from tears to a strange, strained calmness.

"We've got problems," Jed told me, with his talent for front-loading the obvious.

"I don't think so," I said, resisting. "I think Mrs. Garcia has problems."

We called her that 'cause she was like in her forties. Twice as old as Jolie, if not more.

We looked at each other. Jed could have been a movie star. Most of us could have. Not Theodore; he always cramped our style.

I sometimes wondered if The Leader, also handsome, felt a certain competition with Jed. I'm confident in my looks, but any day of the week, I'll tell you The Leader's got more than I do. Jed, however: whole different level.

Jed could make Johnny Depp start slinging poses.

"She'll be arrested, that much I can guarantee." Jed with his smug ex-robber knowledge of the law. "But it's going to cross-pollinate..."

And his smug overgrown vocabulary.

"...between the baby and the rape investigation. You have to wake up, Matthew. There are sixty of us living here. Chicks with four boyfriends who go to sleep with their girlfriends."

I laughed. I liked it. The place was fun. Even the chores.

And I was certain that the fun would not end then.

Only Jed broke with protocol, and that night in my room, he warned me outright that he was going to. I had no rank – only he and The Leader did – but it was somewhat understood that I was something of a third in charge. Everybody liked and listened to me, and The Leader had a habit of lighting up every time I spoke.

"I'm gathering as many as possible to leave," he said.

I had nothing to say to that. It was pure Jed drama. A grand, manic gesture. He probably pictured himself in a slow-motion exodus, leading them all down the street.

But half of these people didn't have jobs. The other half hated the jobs they did have, and had one foot out the office door.

"You're undermining what we've created here," I said. "It's utopic. Don't force it to end just 'cause you think utopias are supposed to."

Jed's eyes showed me that he consented to my depth of debate. From day one, he'd dropped lines about utopias being bound to fail. And given what we all understood about the Law of Attraction, he had to at least wonder if he wasn't willing it to stop working.

"We had a dead infant carried out of here yesterday," he said.

Call me a bastard. Call me insensitive. Call me whatever you want.

But I had to shrug.

It was beside the point. I viewed it as a test. If we could stay glorious beyond this point, I thought, then our entire system was worth preserving.

Sixty

Last Day – 11:57AM

And here I am, now, in the bathroom. Checking the mirror to make sure the remains of my tears have blended into my cheeks.

Glorious.

"But come on, Jed," I say in my mind, my reflection grinning softly as I do. "You can fuck lots of women. You can go cliff-diving. You can even rob stores and get all zonked on adrenaline.

"But you gotta admit, what we're doing here pretty much annihilates everything else."

Talk about adrenaline. And gush? Don't even fucking pretend.

I exist now in a house full of warriors. Scared, yes. Fucking petrified? Of course.

But I'd rather exist amongst their bravery than be the turncoat who topples the kingdom.

I step outside. Here comes Jolie. Her calm, inspiring. We trade rare smiles.

"It's noon," she says, which means it's Downtime. "Should we fuck each other?"

For this woman, I would – I will – lay down and die.

Sixty-One

Edgar Pike's Journal
July, 2009

To ejaculate is to remove eyeglasses. You're in one world before the burst and another one after. Then the prior world grows back. When I was 13, it'd grow back in moments. I'd ejaculate and then want to again. Now, it takes hours to a day to recharge, to get the glasses back on.

At 13, my mother talked everyday about how my armpits smelled. She said that when I was a child, I smelled fresh, but all that was ending. To her, it was as though everything was ending.

Sixty-Two

Last Day – 12:00PM: DOWNTIME

But fucking means motion, and motion means that I can't get any goddamn air. In fact, when I unhook myself from her and roll over to the side, I'm surprised to find that my skin's not cobalt.

The ceiling's wrong. I need to eat. Need to fuck. To stop. Go.

"I think I'm having an asthma attack," I say.

She sits up and regards me, but she's only half-human. The other half is cat. She's writhing; tongue's not inside.

"No, no, you don't have asthma, baby."

Didn't. Just like we didn't have a phone. But I have a phone. It's in my pants, on the dresser. Was I sure to turn it off?

"Since I woke up this morning," I say, but that's not gonna sell her. "Something's wrong with me," I go. "Inside my head."

But you can't say things like that in this house. 'Cause your mind's not in your body here. Your body's probably in your mind. And it's not even your mind, it's the universal mind. Which doesn't matter, anyway, 'cause it probably doesn't exist.

"You're just excited. You're fine. We're almost out of here," she tells me, and did I hear her throat catch on that last part?

I try to touch her with my eyes. Real contact, beyond any sense of murk.

When my next words come, they're not from me (whoever that is). They're from the collective consciousness. They go back all the way to ancient times.

"I want to marry you," I say.

Now she's not a cat. She's gone whole. "I don't know what you're saying," she says, and that effectively makes two of us.

I stand up. Pace. I sit back down. Change positions. My dick's hard (then soft).

"We can marry one another. That's what we're supposed to do."

"Why are we 'supposed to'?"

"'Cause I've only made love to you. That's when you get married."

Would you fucking believe it? I was a virgin before her. Heather in high school went down on me a lot, but that was it. Those two chicks in college came close, but with one I had no condom, and with the other she seemed too drunk and I didn't want to be charged with rape. In the house, there was lots of playfulness, but the fucking only started with Jolie. There was also my cousin Brian in the basement, handful of times, but those were just handjobs, and I was like eleven (twelve, stopped when I was fourteen).

"You do sound different. What's happening, Matthew?"

And now I want to cry again. Thing is, though, my want is all I have. My ducts are shot from before. All I can do is press my heels against my forehead, as though I'm trying to squeeze out a droplet.

"Will you just marry me, okay?" My voice sounds like I'm crying. Eyes still don't look it, though, I'm sure.

"You mean, when? Before tonight?"

Duh. Does she think I'm making high-precision afterlife bets?

"We can ask him to do it. Come on. Right now."

'Cause if I'm moving, I'm good. Walking down the hall, then talking to Him, then doing the ceremony, then lunch, or maybe both at the same time. Hours, hours, hours, minutes, minutes--

She's gone part animal again. She likes it: a look in her eye. Overwhelmed about wedding the one she almost loves.

"How do you think he'll react?" she asks.

Sixty-Three

Last Day – 12:16PM

He, too, is naked. That's how Downtime goes. We tend to pair or group up at that point. For Him it was Beth and Cathleen at the same time. Both are coiled up on His bed. I look at the nightstand: my old-new friend.

Beth seems far away, somehow. Like she's smoking a cigarette and looking out the window, even though she has no cigarette.

Sixty-Four

Edgar Pike's Journal

August, 2009

Orgiastic behavior can make you feel crazy. Enormous adrenaline expended every day. You work yourself up then crash yourself low. Lots of vaginas. All of them disturbing, but I can't get enough. I'm like the man who's eating three sandwiches. On the second one, he gets depressed because soon the third will be gone and he'll be done. The trick is to enjoy the second one!

Sixty-Five

Last Day – 12:17PM

The Leader is on His feet, and He's LOUD:

"If you opened my body, there would be flowers inside of me!"

This: His reaction to being asked to officiate.

Jolie and I make eyes and laugh.

"I'm serious!" He roars. "They are going to find flowers pouring out of me!"

"Oh my God," says Jolie, earnestness wired through her tight. "You're such a poet."

And briefly – half-a-second – I'd like to yell at her.

He turns away from us to pace and think for a moment, and I hope that it's not odd of me to admire His ass's bread-loaf lift.

"What will I say?" He asks, turning back toward us. "I'm afraid I'll mess it up."

Far be it from us to lend Him any advice.

"My talks," He explains, "usually require days of preparation," which is funny since I've seen Him throw more than a dozen together on the spot.

I float Him a smile and, knowing it unwise to counsel Him, decide to band-aid the matter over with: "Well, given the present circumstances, perhaps you'll make an exception."

Everybody in the room, Beth included, ignites with laughter.

Sixty-Six

From THE CULT LEADER'S MIND by Dr. Barry Blumenfeld (pg. 74):

Common to the personalities of most cult leaders is the outward appearance of magnanimity. Stated differently, this is behavior through which the leader can consistently demonstrate his or her generosity. The generosity is typically two-pronged: material and immaterial. Via the material prong, food, housing, and perhaps even monetary allowances are provided, which give the cult members the comfort of childhood yet the absence of authentic freedom. Via the immaterial prong, synthetic generosity of the personality is exhibited. The leader may hold him- or herself up to a high standard in terms of being "open" about his or her true nature, creating something of a confessional environment, in which all the members, the leader included, are encouraged to share intimate details about their pasts, their thoughts, their dreams, and even their deepest secrets. While the leader gathers this information to use against the members, he or she pretends to also share deep information, while in fact submitting to nothing of the sort.

As an example, a leader may "confess" to often feeling guilty about not being able to help all the sick and starving people of the world, but this show of vulnerability is in fact false, leading as it does to a picture of the leader as a being of exceptional generosity and magnanimity.

Sixty-Seven

Last Day – 1PM: LUNCH & THE WEDDING

From the looks of all that food, I kind of hope we can hurry through the "wedding" part. This time, He's gone beyond the fruit. There's bread and ham and sauces overflowing. Five hours to go, I suppose we can risk some metabolic sluggishness.

Jolie has donned a homemade headdress, its white cloth embedded with pink rose petals. Cathleen helped her make it while Beth smiled a certain way.

The Leader's flesh is red as He stands before us. We're all around the table, occupying our assigned seats. My heart's all rat-a-tat-tat, 'cause I know I'll be called up there with Jolie in just a second.

"This is more than a lunch," He says, "because we're going to do something extraordinary."

Jolie and I not only trade smiles, we trade electrical currents.

He says: "You know, when we all came here, I was filled with anger. I know that I don't have a talent for sharing that side of myself, but I had a fire in my mind. Every institution that we all left behind made me angry. From the workforce to the military to the churches to the temples to the schools to the stores to the bars. All of it filled my blood with something harsh. But one institution escaped my wrath."

The creak to my left is Jolie rocking subtly back and forth.

"It escaped my wrath because although it was never something that appealed to me personally, I truly never thought it to be so awful. In fact, if handled with consciousness, it can be quite whole. And on this day, I am delighted beyond belief to share that it appeals to two of our beloved. I am speaking, of course..."

We are putty; He is hands.

"Of marriage."

All our hands, now: raising and slapping together repeatedly.

"And though I never saw a place for myself in marriage, our two young friends have informed me that there is indeed a place for me. Jolie and Matthew, can you please step up here and join me?"

When we do so, we walk not only across the room, but across a silence that could shame the bottom of the ocean.

Instinctively, when before Him, we join hands.

"Well what do we have here?" The Leader yelps. "You two are naturals! I was just going to ask you to do that!"

Beaming. Faces. Each. And. Every. One. Of. Us.

"Now please look deep into each other's eyes, and thus into each other's souls."

His wish = our command.

"Let it be known, in this life and the next, that Matthew and Jolie have found true love with one another.

That in their bravery, they have discarded all things truthless."

"Truthless?" It's me talking. Can't help myself.

"Yes," He says.

"Is that a word?" I ask. (More importantly, is that a smirk I'm wearing?)

Laughter, fearful, from the audience. His hand drops on my shoulder like it's His body part instead of mine.

He whispers yet He's loud and clear: "I didn't have time to get my dictionary!"

The whole group chuckles, myself and Him included.

"They have abandoned," He resumes, "all *things without truth*. They have abandoned all material trappings. They have released the poison of money, of calendars, of corruptible institutions from their lives. And in abandoning these things, they have come to find one another. And so we are gathered here today to unite these two lovers -- these two beautiful, bright souls -- Jolie and Matthew, in the holy, blessed, rapturous union of marriage--"

Sixty-Eight

Last Day – 1:51PM

I didn't go on a honeymoon. I went to the shed.

Surely He's about to kill me. Maybe drop my head in Jolie's lap after, then stand there stoic as the whole group screams.

"This Is What You Get When You Defy Me!" would be His words.

Fuck, I know He hated Jed afterwards. He and I stayed up on more than one night discussing how satisfying it would be – primitive or otherwise – to punch Jed until his skull imploded.

All these tools hanging from the wall. The crowded darkness by way of the lone bulb hanging. Perfect place to die. And I think I'm ready. Moreover, in fact, I'm ready to fight. Come on, let's have it: right here/right now.

Would they all still kill themselves if we never came back inside?

"Okay," He says, "I figured it out."

Deflated: me. He's gone back to the topic of the order. And here I stand all itchy-blooded and panther-like.

"I don't know what my problem was," He says. "I must be distracted. Always remember this: If you're thinking real hard about something, it's not necessarily a good substitute for just letting it come to you."

"When am I supposed to remember that?" I ask.

"What's that?"

"'Always,' you said."

And here He goes all looking into me again.

"If you think your consciousness will end tonight, you're mistaken."

"Sometimes I wonder whether I've ever been conscious," I feel like muttering, but that wasn't muttering; it was the real thing.

"As do I," He grants me, a way of setting us equal.

He steps over to me, puts that Hand-the-size-of-God upon my shoulder.

"We've always related in that regard. A pair of curious cats."

"What's your idea for the order?" I ask (curious panther).

He steps away a bit before He resumes speaking.

"Not only is it simple, but it's consistent with Theodore going third to last. We go in reverse order of our arrival to the group."

I cross my arms. Arms, meet beating heart.

"You see what I'm saying?" He asks me.

"Let me think for a second."

"No thinking." (Naturally.) "It's perfect. Just, think about it: I was first, so I go last. You came second, Theodore third. Then Michael, then the women started: Beth, Cathleen, and Susan. Later was Paul--"

My finger's wagging. "Paul came before Susan."

He goes pensive for a moment, then returns to the outside world. "No, he didn't. He did not. I remember it clearly: three women in a row."

"There wasn't three women, there was four. Allison left."

(Nearly slammed that door off its hinges.)

"Please don't say that name in front of me."

Sixty-Nine

From a C-ABC interview with Allison Roth (11/6/11):

AR: This is a very powerful individual. If most of us hadn't left, he could have taken it to new heights. He could have convinced us that we were on Jupiter instead of Earth, and we would have believed him.

C-ABC: How was he able to be so persuasive?

AR: He controlled us. He controlled every aspect of our lives. Where we slept. What time we woke up and went to bed. Most of the information we consumed. And meditation was very important. We meditated all day long.

C-ABC: Would you say to our viewers that meditation is dangerous?

(Pause.)

AR: If used in the...context of a normal life, then no. Probably no. But within our context it was a tool to silence the mind. Keep the mind very silent. Like a cloud. So you can't pay attention to detail. And the more you do it, it's like a muscle...it keeps on building in that direction.

C-ABC: And regarding the sexual aspects of your relationship with Mr. Pike...was it ever voluntary?

AR: Oh, yes. Of course. Very much so. I initially thought him to be extremely special in that regard. I was very comfortable. We all were.

C-ABC: "We all" meaning all the members?

AR: The women. Most of us. He was not bisexual, as far as I know.

C-ABC: And the charges you've pressed paint the picture of a man who crossed the line...

(Pause.)

AR: Many lines, yes. It began to get violent.

C-ABC: Violent? How--

AR: He would slap us. Choke us. It wasn't in private. He was sometimes with several of us at once. And maybe we did something wrong during the day. Maybe we left a smudge on the mirror. So we'd be in bed, supposedly for a relaxing time, and he'd just start yelling and being very aggressive with his hands. And the rest of himself.

Seventy

Edgar Pike's Journal
May, 2009

I'm realizing the effectiveness of certain words and topics when it comes to recruitment.

The recruitment venue is a source of pride to me. They like us at the yoga center, and have even expressed looking forward to my talks. Call us a "gang," which I'll take. It's fun and cute and light.

Those who come are from varied sectors. Jed is what Malcolm Gladwell calls a Connector; that is, he's good at bringing people together. Every Friday, I'd say 10 percent of the audience is from him, just chatting with strangers on or near the beach. The rest are from New Age sectors; they enjoy yoga, of course, and tantra and meditation. Vegan diets, many of them. A good deal of marijuana users, which is okay. They're impressed when I join them for it; it yields me young.

As of now, we have 23 members. I'd like millions. I think the Internet will have to become involved at some point. Matthew can be of assistance there. He was homeless, briefly, but ironically spent much of his time in the Apple store, surfing the web.

Recruitment doesn't happen during the talks. The talks themselves have a hook regarding Oneness. From Oneness, I go into the Gush. Most of them seem to get it immediately. We then do meditations right there, and all of them get it.

They see, meditating, that there's the gush -- which is always running hot; all our instincts and feelings and drives and rhythms and aliveness -- and then there's the hum...

You CAN ACTUALLY Separate The Two. At any moment.

Once you see that you can divide them, you see that both are illusions. I speak in support of the gush, which is where much of life's pleasures reside. The hum, however, I speak of as more real, since it's foundational and identical within every single one of us.

But real recruitment happens after, during snacks and juice. I speak to the women, primarily, though lend courtesy to the men. Our discussions are primarily about the sermon. Some say "lecture," which is okay.

Then I'll use words. It shames me when I fail and delights me when I succeed.

One such word is "tits." I will speak to a woman for a long enough time, get her to like me, then use "tits" in a given context, usually in pursuit of humor. If she doesn't like it, I discard the exchange. If she deems it funny or proceeds unimpeded, then I know she is of a sufficiently sexual nature to warrant further engagement, either then or in the future.

Blushing, I talk of "mooning," too. Of how, for example, Laura in the group thinks it's funny to moon the rest of us. This is a good topic, safer than tits, because unlike the above, it straddles the line between sexuality and sheer silly humor. Still, a woman can give herself away through her reaction to the topic. If she likes it, sufficient sexuality has been discovered. If she's tight, I have no remaining use.

These are sophomoric games; I'll be the first to admit it. But like the low word I dislike, they get at the root of our basic truth. Pleasure centers. Gush. Not to be dismissed, unreal though it is, essentially.

Seventy-One

Last Day – 1:53PM

Him: "Anyway, four in a row, whatever, but Paul was later."

"No. I met him before we met Susan."

"Maybe, okay, fine. But I met him after I met Susan."

"So we're going with who you met or who a given group representative met?"

"I guess me. It makes no difference."

"It'll make a difference when we're all standing there at six o'clock."

Some space grew between us as we spoke, but He narrows it, His footsteps hard on the floor.

"I've lost a lot of people this year," He says. "Am I going to lose you, too?"

Till now, I thought gulping was a thing of myth. But here I go, Adam's apple clicking.

"Interesting choice of words," I say, my mouth a humid hollow. "Talking about loss."

"What's that supposed to mean?"

I look into His (computer salesman) eyes.

"Matthew?"

But I say: "I'm fine. You're not gonna lose me."

He releases some air. Now He's touching my face, the expression of which works hard not to change. I've got ground to hold, and it goes like this:

"But you realize what this means?" I say to Him.

He waits.

"It means Jolie's now going first."

Seventy-Two

Last Day – 1:54PM

"What do you want from me?" He says in return, only He doesn't verbalize those words; He makes them come to life by sighing and letting His palms go even with the ceiling.

What He actually says is: "All the more reason to make sure we move quickly."

And then He's done with me again, which is to say He's gone from the shed.

The light and green and blue flood in and ice me.

I hear music coming from the house, drums (keep drumming) and bells and flutes and pipes and strings. All of them by way of a CD player that He usually keeps locked in a closet off the kitchen. Every day, though, right before two, He brings it out to spur the Ecstatic Dance.

I watch Him go across the lawn, the mathematics of His motives so clear as to be startling. Jolie was afraid of the knives, so He punished both of us by putting Theo third to last instead of her. Then, as a way to hide His motives and keep us docile, He oversaw our wedding, becoming a proponent of an institution that (believe it) He's always hated.

Then, to stick the knife in deeper – and having gained some ground by marrying us – He put Jolie first in the goddamn order.

His reasons? Only God can know.

Which to Him is no invasion of privacy, since He thinks He is God.

To me, however, as I watch Him go up the steps, He's looking more and more like some kind of man.

Seventy-Three

Last Day – 1:55PM

And I may be but a boy, but I think it's time to start stabbing this man back.

Seventy-Four

From BREAKING NEWS L.A.'s exclusive interview with Jed Bracken (10/12/11):

Look, I was the closest guy to him, save for maybe Matt Barrett, and I can't say with certainty that I ever knew what he was really thinking. That's the whole fucking point! You know what he's thinking, you may as well go home.

Nah, fuck that. You gotta stick around! On Tuesday, he seems mad at you for some strange reason, then on Wednesday all of a sudden he's giving you a hug and calling you his "son." So on Tuesday you want to blow your brains out, but on Wednesday you could climb a fuckin' mountain with no gear! So you want more of that Wednesday feeling, all the time! But on Thursday he's fuckin' pissed off 'cause his soup is cold. So you spend Friday-Saturday-Sunday trying to appease him. Nothing, right? But Monday! Oh, man. Monday he starts telling like ten other people how handsome he thinks you are. And your blood gets all juicy. You're a god.

So when you feel like a god, you don't want to know what he's thinking! You just want to keep feeling like a god. He'll be giving a goddamn sermon, and you're half-listening but you believe everything he's saying – because, fuck, hey, at least he's not mad at you right now! And if he is mad, who cares? Forgive him. Wait for him. Because come tomorrow, you just might be his son again.

You getting any of this?

Seventy-Five

Last Day – 2PM: ECSTATIC DANCE

I go across the lawn. This is it. Far be it from me to know my own nature, but I'm sensing that it's not some loose conglomeration of obedient parts.

I'm sensing instead that it doesn't like a wall against its back.

Which is fitting since I have wind at my back, and it pushes me in through the home's rear door, whereupon I'm greeted by holy music and dancing bodies and guzzled wine.

Energy like this: relentless. It's a compulsion with compulsiveness as its goal (keep drumming).

But I'm about to take the moving entity that is Jolie, and snap her into a freeze so tight it'll choke her.

She comes up to me. Kisses me. Lips like the rose petals about her head.

My mouth, however, doesn't kiss her back. It gives her words:

"He wants you to go first," it says, and I watch the words settle upon her gray matter like fallen feathers.

No more dancing. No more moving.

She looking at me/me looking at her.

But then her eyes go perfectly closed. Whatever's behind them, I cannot say. His words from the Group Talk Session, maybe?

Whatever it is, it gets her dancing anew.

And by the time I turn away, having sneered, her dance is twice as ecstatic as before.

Seventy-Six

Last Day – 2:06PM

Okay, Jed, you fucking dweeb: It's you and me, so let's get used to it.

Door locked. Sink on. Phone dialed.

He answers with that voice that I'd love to punch: "Matthew?"

"You left us." I'm sneering so hard I'll need a dentist. "The pressure was absolutely fucking insane, and you guys just left one night."

"I'm sorry, Matthew."

"How am I supposed to trust you if you left?"

"Would you rather trust the person who's for life, or the one who's for death--?"

"Yeah, yeah, yeah, I know the fucking argument already. I've been through it. But why should I trust *you*?"

The silence of the Jed.

"It's already the afternoon," Jed says. "If we knew your location--"

"No! I swear to God, I will hang up this phone. I'm out on a limb like you can't even imagine."

"He doesn't love you, Matthew."

And here's The Leader's special magic. Here's me defending The Man with force: "That man sacrificed everything for us. He had a life, he made money. Do you know how long he cried after you went?"

"He's not a well person, Matthew."

"You knew Ascension was possible for years."

"Matthew, he only really started mentioning it when he fell under scrutiny--"

"Stop saying my name over and over--"

"He's just not brave enough to kill himself by himself--"

More wordplay like that and I'll kill myself now.

"That's all well and good," I say. "But he's never walked out on me. He's never lied to me."

And that's the thing about The Leader. That's why His hooks form such ambitious curls. All that fucking truth and loyalty. Head games, sure. But Jed's a whole other form of person.

"He has," Jed says.

"Which?" I ask. "Walked out or lied?"

"Lied!"

"I'm not talking about little things."

"Matthew--"

"*What*?"

"Did you hear my messages?"

"No."

Jed: "He's been sexual with Jolie."

And at this point, as if I haven't already, I lose my fucking mind--

"You're a liar!" I scold him. "You've always lied!"

"Ask him."

"*I hope your life is a fucking mess. I'll put a goddamn curse on you.*"

"Ask both of them."

I throw my back against the bathroom door, so hard it's like I expect a stampede to come through.

And Jed starts up with: "We can help you start all over again. Your whole life. Matthew?"

Too much of that name. I shut the phone.

I feel like a guy who's got violence where his soul belongs.

Seventy-Seven

Edgar Pike's Journal
May, 2009

Did Laura think she could continue her behavior without an occurrence such as tonight's? It's getting to the point where barely two days can pass without her lowering her britches and exposing her rear end to somebody. She is "known" for it, now. It makes my blood start to jump, and I imagine many of ours.

So now she's embarrassed and it's awkward between us, because I made a display of ejaculating on her hindquarters. Beth was near to us, and Angela, and one of them said I was "marking my territory," which was solid humor.

It was a natural extension of her exhibitionism. Tears can flash in her eyes and she can pretend she's not talking to me, but I don't see her packing her bags. And I refuse to bother with feelings of guilt or shame.

It was a jolting, tender shot. And I love her. And I think I'll have another when I see who's awake.

Seventy-Eight

Last Day – 2:24PM

I'm having trouble squaring how He taught us so much about action with the fact that I can only think in miniature steps.

Certainly a confrontation with Jolie is essential.

And certainly it'd be excessive to pull her from the dance by her hair, so I take her by the hand as though we're friends, then I lead her toward the hallway, even shaking a little bit to the music to show that I'm into it.

Before I did so, she was dancing with Theodore, a pairing that would have seemed satirical if anything in the world were still funny.

When I have her alone, in the hallway off the living room, I sense excitement rising up inside of her, as though I'm about to kiss her privates, privately.

But when she sees the look on my face, she's smart enough to ask, "What is it?"

It's not too late to check back in. Phone in the drawer, right where I found it. Jed never the wiser as to where we are. Sundown. Us down. Destiny articulated.

Yet I'm holding the sun up with both hands. "Has he ever had you?" I say to her.

And then I try to read her face, which is as legible as Sanskrit scratched into the dirt.

"Don't lie to me," I say to her, as if that will inspire a surge of truth.

"I don't know what you're talking about."

I do her the courtesy of making it clear: "Have you ever let him fuck you?"

Now she's legible: eyes wide, mouth open. "What the fuck are you asking me right now?"

"If you keep delaying--"

"You're asking me if I fucked him?"

My breath is getting to know her eyes.

"I'll know it in your face if you're lying to me," I bluff.

"You're scaring the shit out of me right now."

"You're scaring the fucking shit out of me. Where the hell are you right now?"

"What? With you."

"I mean in your head." I poke my own head with my finger, making blotches appear before my eyes. "You're off somewhere else."

She's now gonna do what The Leader never has: she sets about abandoning me, tries to walk away. But like-that my hand's around her elbow: clammy (both).

"Like being fake or something," I go on.

"We're involved in something special here. If you can't give in to it—"

"Now you even sound like him. And smell like him. In your breath!"

She tries and tries to get away.

"I would never do that." She starts to cry. "You know he's like a father to me, and you know what my real father did!"

Those last words breaking down, all boo-hoo-hoo, which is what I say:

"Oh, boo-hoo-hoo. So now I'm supposed to not say anything, right?"

"Let go of me."

I'm roaring now: "You're so fucking transparent!"

"*Let go of me*!"

Right on cue, here comes The Leader. Fear rips through me: calves to backs-of-lungs.

I let go.

"You have to talk to him," Jolie cries to Him.

She turns the corner. If she resumes dancing this time, I'll be impressed.

The way The Leader looks at me, it seems inevitable that the bullshit meter is going to have to relax a notch. How long can we keep on veiling the tension? Pretending to mistake His madhouse for a well-oiled machine?

"What's going on here?" He asks me.

Where does one begin...

"She's crying?" He asks me.

The obvious: stated.

And then He lets me down by punting.

"Jolie!" He says, and He starts to go after her.

"Don't go after her," I command Him.

He spins back toward me. "What demon is inside you, Matthew?"

What demon isn't?

"I'm going to ask you a question now," I tell Him.

"Anything, Matthew. I don't understand--"

"Do you..." (Just breathe.)

The Leader's eyes are orbs.

"...keep secrets from us?"

"Truly, I don't know what you mean."

"Truly, you do."

"You're hurting me, Matthew." And His eyes are moist. "You can't know how your behavior is making me feel."

My lungs produce a windstorm of breath.

"I have nothing but love for you," The Leader says.

"Do you hide things from me?" I ask.

Partial translation: I don't love you back.

The Leader touches my wrist. I try to resist, but I meet with His strength.

"Come with me now," He says to me.

I try and try to get away.

"What are you going to do?" I ask Him.

But we're going toward the living room, toward the others, and it's obvious.

"You can't have them," I say. "I'm asking you a question."

"We're a family. Come on."

I roar: "This is private!"

* * *

"That's private," I said to my cousin Brian, as he undid my belt buckle and began to lower my pants.

"It's not private if I show you mine, too," he explained.

Everything in my head knew it not to be right, but the way his words came into me, they somehow kept managing to make me stop protesting.

Till it got to the point where there was one me inside, screaming for him to stop, and another me outside, acting like I liked it.

Seventy-Nine

Last Day – 2:28PM

The Leader:

"*Turn off the goddamn music*!"

Everybody stops dancing, which was what Jolie was doing when we came in: not dancing. She's gone from the room, actually. Score one for her sanity, I guess.

The music doesn't stop immediately. It pounds on, its rapture a farcical thing.

Beth crosses to the stereo and fiddles with it. The Leader watches her hands, as if trying to will them to touch the right buttons. At long last, she achieves overwhelming silence.

Our eyes all make contact as His yell still echoes through us.

"I'm sorry," He says. Another first. "Forgive me. I didn't mean to be abrasive."

The Leader looks around.

"Where is Jolie?"

All eyes start searching with the exception of mine. Wherever she is, it beats being in my sight.

"Somebody go to her room."

It's Paul who does the honors.

We wait. The Leader realizes that His hand's still clamped around my wrist. He lets go. My wrist crunches. It would hurt bad if everything else didn't.

"We're having a meeting," He says. "Something's wrong in this house."

"Yeah, I agree," I whisper.

"Please be quiet now," He orders.

All of us wait for Jolie's reappearance.

After an eternity, Paul returns with her in tow. Jolie's eyes meet only the floor. Her face bears blotches like the ones in my head.

"Jolie, are you all right?" asks The Leader.

Everybody looks at her. The attention makes her seem to shrink.

Jolie nods once, says, "Thank you, yes."

After nodding His approval, The Leader says, "Please, now, let us all form a circle."

We have ourselves another first: a collective moment of hesitation.

"I apologize again for raising my voice. I promise it won't happen again."

That does it. We're a circle, jerk. Everyone joins hands. Since I'm still next to Him, His hand's in mine. My wrist bites itself at His touch, a kind of allergy.

"I know that everybody was enjoying the music," He says, "and I hope that that enjoyment not only continues, but grows larger and fuller as the evening nears."

Nods of understanding occur atop stiff necks.

"But, alas, we have to conduct a bit of work. It appears that Matthew has a question for us."

My volume knob is way low: "For you."

He looks at me. His hand twitches. I sense He'd like to squeeze mine harder.

"If it's for me, well, then, it's for me, and I'll be happy to answer it in front of the whole group."

Oh, forgive me if I haven't introduced myself: I'm the Center of Attention. And as The Leader has known well for years, I so hate being myself.

"I'm not sure you want to do this this way," I say.

"Matthew!" (Wow! Could've done without that!) "You are a wise and capable assistant. But I am certain that I want to do this this way."

I give Jolie a rueful look. My girl. She cries. This goddamn place.

"Do you..." I begin.

But my words short out.

"It's okay, Matthew. There is love in this circle."

Still, nothing. Just a boy and a bunch of shakes.

He then says: "I'm sorry, how thoughtless of me. Would you like to stand beside your lovely wife?"

The mention of our union makes Jolie cry harder.

"It's okay," I say, shaking my tired head.

And I guess I now find myself checked back in. 'Cause what's a boy to do but take the silly order? I suck in so much air that I hope there's enough left over for everyone else.

"Do you," I say, "relate to Jolie...with your body?"

I'm pretty sure the sweat on my palms isn't mine.

Jolie is the next to express herself, though she does so in sobs instead of words.

"Oh, Matthew..." says The Leader.

Here He goes.

"Oh, Matthew. What pain you have put within my heart. Can you feel it running through your hand?"

Again, I give a shake of my head.

"I can't feel you," I say. "I don't know you."

"You don't what?" His words are fired through with concern.

"I don't know you." I try to clear my throat, but whatever's in there feels painted on. "Please, what is the answer?"

The Leader looks at Jolie, who by now could use a bucket at her feet.

"It was our understanding," He says, "that Jolie was to lay only with you."

"That was our understanding," I say.

"And she has laid...only with you!"

Relief tickles at me, but so what? The fuck else would this guy say? Am I to be the kind of kid who's awed when the weatherman predicts the sunrise?

The Leader looks at Jolie: "Jolie?"

"I would..." She's shaking. "Never lie to you, Matthew."

"Nor would I," says The Leader.

I view my hand, tucked inside of His. Looking mighty white.

I pluck it. He retracts His.

"Are those acceptable answers for you, Matthew?" He wants to know.

"I think that I need to get some rest," I say.

The Leader nods. He's coming at me. Slow: a glide. His lips kiss my forehead, not minding the sweat.

Barking out a sound of relief, The Leader says, "I think everybody could use some rest. We'll need energy for the journey."

I look at Jolie.

When she looks back at me, my heart (for once) could stop.

"So let's everybody go to our rooms," He says. "We'll resume for the Eternity Chant at four. There is a time for togetherness, and a time to be alone."

Eighty

Edgar Pike's Journal

June, 2011

Monastery? Could I bear it?

Eighty-One

Last Day – 2:48PM

But alone, for us, means alone together.

Which makes me think that He's maybe not lying. Why else would He allow us to be in our room conversing? Or does He just not care?

Does the coming journey supercede the drama?

Maybe, in His mind, the journey supercedes the order, too.

Which makes me just a kid who's been freaking out. Delusions of Grandma dancing in my head.

I smile.

This as I meditate. Jolie's in the shower. Was He who taught me how to meditate, and now the practice is helping me calm down.

Was that a trick? He taught me how to be calm so I wouldn't question Him?

A soft cloud rolls over the thought.

I'm empty.

Nothing.

Nobody.

Like everyone else.

Calm – the – fuck – down, Matthew.

If you view the scoreboard, you know the following:

Jed: proven liar. Said he'd stay forever. Didn't.

Leader: a petty fuck, sometimes, and annoying, but come on – What's the guy ever done? Made it so my girl would die forty seconds before me? Am I fucking kidding?

"He's not good," Jolie says, and the words are so foreign from the realm of her mouth that her voice sounds nothing like hers at all.

My eyes open. She's fresh from the shower, has an aura made of steam.

"What?" I ask her.

"I think he..."

She pauses. A pause so long that it has ambitions to become a stop.

"...might not be good."

I think of Allison and Laura, running from the house.

A flame spikes upward within my being.

"What do you mean?" I ask her, and she sits down beside me on the floor.

* * *

It was a weekend that, for me, represented us in our prime.

I even recall liking Jed that weekend. Somehow, I was able to tuck in my envy and roll with him. I was in the backseat, behind the passenger seat, which means I was the one who Jed's eyes kept going to as he spoke from behind the wheel.

Paul rode shotgun. Jolie to my left.

And Jed launched into one of his you're-not-gonna-fucking-believe-this stories. That's what Jed is like. His stories are better than yours. The friends he hears them from are cooler than yours, and certainly cooler than you. The guy's got friends in prison, for Christ's sake. He's got access to a realm that you and me would piss our pants in.

Thing is, in real life, when somebody tells you they're about to hit you with some colossal, mind-blowing story, they usually fail to. Maybe it's funny in theory, or it has a good middle, but usually the goods don't get delivered.

Jed – the motherfucker – is an exception to this rule. He gets launching, and despite everything in me, I actually sit up and get ready to listen. And when I do listen, I do so closely, hoping to memorize the details and rhythms for the sake of passing it on.

Which I'll attempt to do right now.

I don't recall where the fuck he got this thing from. I was stoned off my ass and Jolie's thigh was showing from beneath her skirt. Which is not to say that I wasn't listening, but that my brain somehow managed to lurch upright for the good parts.

Which were:

"There was a college class, somewhere in America," said Jed.

Stop me if you've heard this one.

"A professor of, I think, philosophy. Maybe even literature, but it doesn't matter. The point is, he taught the kids real hard, you know? He drove those kids. All year long, they got their faces dragged through the dirt."

That made me laugh, not 'cause it was funny, but 'cause it was so unnecessarily intense, like Jed himself. (And my brain, right then, too. What was in that herb?)

"And when it came time for finals," said Jed, "he made them study their fucking asses off. Gave them a reading list that would make you puke. Kept dropping little hints about what a fucking total disaster this test would be, and how low the odds were of any single one of them passing it."

Michael I saw in the side-view mirror, a smile giving his face a lift.

"And those kids were scared. I mean they were studying all night. Not all of them, of course, but most of them. Balls to the wall. Getting together in groups. Doing whatever they could to ace all this material..."

"Come on, pal," Michael says, his smile prohibiting any tension whatsoever. "You gotta get to the point or I'm gonna strangle you."

We all laughed.

Jed said, "You strangle me, we all go off this fucking mountain."

'Cause we were heading north of Santa Barbara, to a cabin that The Leader kept God-knows-where with God-knows-what-money.

And leave it to Jed to dish snappy comebacks, which made all of us laugh even harder, looking over the lethal edge, Jed driving in the maniac way that ex-cons are supposed to, and me, Jolie, and Michael proving ourselves, unbeknownst to ourselves, to be perfect candidates for Ascension by way of our glee.

Ironic since Jed was the one driving.

This was, I want to say, about ten months ago.

So Jed wasn't about to speed things up, but I did get the sense, when he continued, that he actually had been near to the point before Michael tried to get him moving.

"Comes test day," he said, "and everyone's real, real nervous. Nobody has to say anything, 'cause it's too known: This is do or die. They've been through the whole universe..."

Michael shook his head, smile stretching.

"They had explored all the great philosophers, and tried to map the grid of the universe, and attempted to explain what mankind was about, and all grown close, and fallen in love with the teacher, and now it was time to put all that data to use.

"So the teacher's got this look on his face, right?"

And when Jed says "right," the word is loaded up with so much coolness that it becomes a contagion and makes you say (or at least mouth) "right," as well.

He went, "He's looking at all of them like he knows something they don't. And these poor kids are shitting their pants. And the teacher passes out the test, which is on a single sheet of paper, and tells them all to keep their copies face-down till he tells them otherwise."

"Was it blank?" Jolie asks, 'cause that's Jolie: She searches her decks for Jokers, all life long.

"No," said Jed, "but that's a good guess. Wasn't blank. Anyway, everybody got their copy, and the teacher went up to the front of the room and crossed his arms, let them simmer a little more, and finally said, 'Okay, turn your papers over...'

"Upon the page was no place to put your name, no place to put the date, no lines...just a single question..."

"Fuck," said Michael.

I was in a trance.

"'WHY?'" said Jed, and I'm pretty sure his ensuing chuckle was natural.

"The only word," he said, "on the test was Why? And these guys had to harness all their knowledge to answer it."

I couldn't believe any of this. Dead or not, famous or not, Jed surely belonged in some kind of museum.

"So everybody starts to write down their answers, right?"

"Right," said me and Jolie and Michael.

"And they're going on and on for paragraphs. Throwing in every fucking thing they can remember. Religion, science, philosophy. Facts, theories, quotes, angles, arguments. They're going for it. They're covering all sides.

"It went on all period, and it was a special period, a couple hours, I think..."

Not casual enough to pass as nonfiction, but it did lend some depth to the mounting intensity.

"And in the end – guess what? Nearly every single kid in that class got an F."

"No!" said Jolie, the injustice rattling her.

"Yes!" Jed smiled. Those eyes in the rear-view. "Only one dude managed to get a passing score, and that dude got an A.

"Can you guess what he said?"

We surely couldn't. All our philosophy books had long been sealed shut, tucked away, and replaced by what The Leader told us.

"WHY NOT?!" Jed yelled, one finger aimed upward. "And that motherfucker walked out of there in two minutes. Got the A. 'Why not?'"

For months thereafter, my brain would whisper: *He said "Why not?" and walked out of the room.*

I'd be in the shower, be scraping tiles, and out of nowhere, inside, amid silence: *He said "Why not?" and walked out of the room.*

Michael, however, wasn't buying it. The truth of the tale, he didn't much care about, but within moments, he began to pick at its simple poetry.

"That's bullshit!" he said, his smile intact and operational.

Jed laughed. They were friendly, these two, and their debates tended to reach new heights when an audience was involved.

Smiling, too, Jolie and I ably fulfilled the role.

"Why is that bullshit?" Jed asked Michael.

"'Cause it's clever enough to paper over real thought, but you take away the paper and there ain't much there."

"Bro!" Jed yelled, instantly exasperated. "I give you a fucking story that encapsulates the essence of mankind, the essence..."

Michael smiled on.

"...of staying alive, of existing, of going forward, and you tell me it's 'papered over'? Whatever the fuck that means?"

"It means that 'why not' is a cop-out. 'Why not' sounds all *carpe diem* and shit, but that's an unconscious way to live your life."

"That's the only way to live your life!"

Keep drumming.

"You're never gonna find the answer," Jed continued. "You're never gonna crack the mystery. In the end, it's gonna boil down to 'might as well.'"

"Bullshit!" Michael was a notch too loud, even by the standards of sound entertainment. "You don't have to crack the mystery. That's not the fucking point. But you do have to engage with it. You do have to establish some kind of code, some kind of way to go about living your life."

"You just walked right into that," Jed yelled. Jolie and I sprang forward, laughing. "'Why not' is nothing if not a code."

“But it’s a teenager’s code. It’s a code you get in a cereal box. Have you listened to what Master says?”

“Of course! Have YOU listened to what Master says? He never comes in for landing, that guy. It’s always open-ended. It’s a work in progress. We’re all engaged in an experiment.”

“Yet more things are to come,” said Michael. “He always hints at it. More is coming. Ascendant consciousness. Where there’s that, there has to be more than your fucking ‘why not.’”

It occurred to me, watching them, that even though their predominant motive was to be playful, they were like a microcosm of everything that’s wrong with the world. The fact that everywhere you go, no matter where you are geographically or historically, you come upon people that have certain systems, and, whether they intend to be or not, are the staunch and natural defenders of those systems.

The artist: “Where would we be without art?”

The doctor: “Where would we be without medicine?”

Scientist: “Where would we be...?”

But none of these people want to take it all. The artist and the scientist throw sneers back and forth. They need each other, but they wag their dicks, and they don’t have to be male to do so.

Anyway, the “debate” rolled on: Why?/Why not?/ Why?/Why not?

I spoke up only once. I said, "You know, Camus said the only real philosophical question is whether or not we should kill ourselves."

The car went silent. Admittedly, I had gone too heavy. Jed's rear-view eyes went searching for meaning. Then he said, "We know, Matthew. Master talks about that, like, every day."

At which point all the weight was gone, and everybody laughed (and I pretended to).

And that's why Jed is Jed and I am me: He tells you real fucking stories and I just repeat what I've heard.

* * *

They decided to put the premise before The Leader. When we got to the cabin, there were easily twenty people there, and the ghost of pot-just-smoked making its way up toward the ceiling. The Leader, He never indulged too much; He liked to stay sharper than the rest of us, even if only by an inch.

"Good," Jed said when we walked in, "you're smoking. That'll help you help us."

And I watched that fucking guy tell the whole college professor story again, probably with ninety-eight percent the same language, pauses, and turns of phrase, and still, despite my repeat exposure, I was near-to-entirely certain that I could never tell it even half that well.

Moreover, Jed got the entire room going: girls wanting to watch and hear him/guys wanting, generally, to become him. The Leader didn't seem to mind; what use was a second in charge if he didn't have weight to throw around?

At the end, Jed gave Michael like four seconds to stutter out his piece, after which they asked The Leader which side He was on.

But here's what I knew that Jed never could: The Leader would never, ever take sides when given an equation such as that one. Was Jed fucking kidding? Like he'd said himself, The Leader was a movable piece. Never did a block of chessboard settle underneath Him for too long.

He proved my instincts within two seconds: "Why should one have to choose?" He asked.

"Because," Jed said, quieter than he was in the car but no less forceful for it, "it's a fundamental choice. It's not thin or shallow. We're talking about taking the questioning stance or the active stance."

The Leader let out a gallant laugh. "Can an active person not be a questioner? Can a questioner not be active? I sense boxes."

Everybody smiled.

The residue from their toke was sifting into me. I looked at Jolie and sensed a box myself. She knew me, smiled.

"No boxes!" Jed yelled, his own smile ensuring that we'd all be fine if the power were to suddenly go out.

“Doesn’t have to be boxes. Can be leanings. Can be a preference.”

“Preferences lead to boxes.” The Leader shrugged.

“Am I not your second-in-command?” Jed asked, never one to shy away from some post-modern self-awareness.

“Certainly you are.”

“Okay, so somewhere in there, like it or not, worse or better, is the presence of preference.”

Some of the faces absorbed this line with unease, but I didn’t catch The Leader doing any heel-rocking, and I was positive that He’d come back strong.

“Not preference,” said The Leader. “Just utility.”

“OH!” This was Michael.

Lots of others grinned.

“You sure know how to hurt a guy,” said Jed, the muscles beneath his thin shirt indicating a man who could in no way – ever – be hurt.

The Leader barked laughter. “Come on, stop it. You’re good at your job. That’s all I’m saying. That needn’t mask some sickly hierarchy.”

“Are YOU not at the top of this hierarchy?”

Now things were getting ever-so-slightly tense.

“What hierarchy?” The Leader seemed lost.

“The one...” Jed’s finger aimed itself at the carpet and made circles like the Earth ‘round the sun. “...of which we’re all a part.”

“You want a hierarchy,” said The Leader, “go back to the world. All I am is a shaman orchestrating truth. You want it, you can have it. You don’t, you can ignore it. Correct?”

He looked at all of us. We nodded as fast as our heads allowed.

“So that says to me,” Jed said to The Leader, “that you’re on the side of ‘why not?’”

“Why?” asked The Leader, knowing full well that the inquiry was funny right at that moment. “Aside from the fact that position-holders always project their own values onto others.”

“You’re on the side of ‘why not,’” said Jed, ignoring the dig, “‘cause you just roll with things. You said so now. Hear me, don’t hear me. Stay, leave. Whatever. Why not?”

The Leader paused.

I saw Him thinking. I could not sense whether His thoughts were laced with anger.

Eighty-Two

Edgar Pike's Journal
March, 2009

Sometimes I hate Jed.

The problem is, he's intuitive. He's not good with information, facts, or history. He writes with his left hand, which means his right brain is in control. That's imagination, poetry, creativity. Good with words, like I, which is why we're a fit.

I hate him, though, because his intuition comes on me like a rude palm. Lands and touches. "GROSS!" (I put quotes because Allison said that today, while cleaning hair from the drain.)

I'm standing there clean, and Jed will look at me too close. Then I feel unclean. Like his look has created a ripple.

It's a good test, though. To withstand that. I must be clean.

Eighty-Three

Last Day – Matthew Thinking Back

"If I had to choose..." said The Leader, and every eyeball at the party went wide. "And that's a very big if..."

"I know," said Jed, the fisherman with a tug tightening his line.

"...then I would actually have to side with Michael."

Michael made a victorious sound, something between an "Oh!" and an "Ah!" and walked over to The Leader and gave Him five. The Leader, as one could expect, played along, the look on His face expressing that He deemed the gesture rather inane.

Jed's beam of confidence was still wholly accounted for. He watched The Leader with glass-cutting reverence, waiting for Him to say His final piece.

"Reason being," said The Leader, "that why? is open. Why is a door. Why not is an attitude. Why is what drives me being 'whatever,' as you say. Because I work to accept all extremes. I live with the perception that my essence is larger than I can possibly imagine. As is yours. And everyone's. So that to me looks like a why.

"After all," The Leader then said with a wink, "look what that why did to all the students. Got them all thinking and writing and expressing themselves. Sounds like a good professor, asking a question like that. But not a very good grader, if he's to reward the one who gives back shallowness."

At which point Jed went and toasted his beer (how and when it got into his hand, I don't know), and gave up the whole thing like the gentleman that he is.

However, I didn't give it up. I found myself sucked into an undertow of sadness. Jolie disappeared, went into a room somewhere, and I didn't even want to find her.

I felt like The Leader had betrayed me. Not only by giving an actual answer, but by choosing the one liked by Michael. At that moment, I felt like every single thing I'd heard Him say and seen Him do had been misinterpreted.

The goddamn drum circle – had I misread that? I thought the gush and the flow were the thing. But now He was weighing in with a "Why?"

And frankly, I didn't want to know why. I liked the kid from Jed's epic story. If we're bigger than we can imagine, how could we ever shake a good answer out of why? Don't we instead have to roll with our lives, and essentially stick with why not?

Or maybe the truth is, as The Leader initially tried to say, that why is no different from why not. Both are inquiries. Both actually knock on doors. And both have shapes that are hard to see clearly.

Still, I didn't like that He took that position. Given the fact that He took any at all, I would have preferred the opposite, or alternative, or what have you.

So I got drunk.

I wanted to unload my mind. Not unleash its contents, unload its presence. No mind for a night. Too much of it, anyway. Mind-mind-mind – where's it get you, ever?

To the cooler, I kept returning for one beer after another. I'm reasonably certain that I drank more than most others. Hopefully nobody saw what I was up to. And certainly nobody related to my crisis, as everybody was having a pretty regular old party, collected in little groups to talk or smoke or drink or fuck.

I even saw The Leader and Jed laughing together.

Why?

'Cause I guess that whole conversation had just been theater to them.

Why?

'Cause I guess they figured it was a party and there was no need to get all uptight.

Why?

'Cause weekdays were the time for getting uptight, and this was supposed to be a special break.

Why?

'Cause we worked so hard during the goddamn week, and this week had been special, 'cause we'd painted the house, and I didn't know about everybody else but my ribs still felt crushed.

Why?

'Cause my parents and I hadn't talked in two years, and living amongst this beauty and meaning was a far better deal than searching garbage cans for pizza crust on Santa Monica Boulevard.

Why?

Have you not listened to a word I've said?

Why not?!

I spun. A pinball within the gears of the cabin. Half a conversation here, one-tenth of a garbled flirtation there.

Jolie, where?

I didn't know/didn't care.

Kept bouncing. Head in a cartwheel that had lost its hinges.

Why?

Fuck you.

That's why. It's my goddamn life.

* * *

And I don't know what that night was made of. Beyond the debating, I don't know what incidents and exchanges and revelations defined that night. I certainly gained nothing shy of confusion. For me, prime or otherwise, it was a lost event, and the whole sad time, Jolie was lost, too.

At times, I even thought we were about to break up.

I'd turn corners, stick my head into rooms, expecting/intuiting her to be there, but finding other faces staring back.

Eighty-Four

Last Day – 2:57PM

And today, as our hours fold themselves away for good, she's here on the floor of our bedroom telling me

In plain words

That she's pretty sure The Leader touched her that night.

Eighty-Five

Last Day – 2:58PM

Why?

Ask Him.

If He were as drunk as I was at the time, He'd probably be honest and say, "Why not?"

Eighty-Six

Last Day – 3PM: SECOND DOWNTIME (ECSTATIC DANCE INTERRUPTED; SECOND CHORES CANCELLED)

"He came into my room that night," she says. "The only night when you weren't with me."

My hands leave my lap and turn into fists. They stay so when I plant them on the floor.

"He's come into our room," I say, being fair. "He likes to check on us."

"Wasn't that. He was there for a long time. I haven't really thought about it. But he was there. I know that for a fact. I don't have any idea for how long, because I was mostly asleep the whole time."

"Mostly asleep?"

"Usually I'm on guard. But I smoked a lot that night. And Janice was still with us, then, and she made, like, cookies with weed, also. So I was deep asleep, but, like, waking up in little pieces. And I know he was there with me, and I know he was right near the bed. But I can't say a hundred percent whether or not he touched me."

"What percent can you say?"

She thinks. Her mouth moves. She then says, "Maybe fifty."

The odds of a successful marriage.

"What'd he look like?" I want to know, switching from numerical data to visual.

“Just like himself.” She thinks me dumb.

“But, like...” Whatever calmness the meditation lent me has been retracted. “...what was the expression on his face? Did he seem...turned on or something?”

“Hmm...”

I see that this is hard for her. Not only mentally, in terms of remembering, but ethically, in terms of incriminating.

And I know He’s either downstairs or in His room, trusting that when we see Him next we’ll be more manageable.

I then recall the clank from hours ago.

“There was something still about him,” Jolie shares. “He wasn’t in a rush.”

Was the clank a gun?

She goes on, “I remember feeling safe for a minute, like I was happy to have him there. But then he got closer -- and I remember a question forming in my mind. Just now, in the shower, I was trying to figure out what the question was.”

“Did you?”

“I couldn’t nail it down completely. But it was something to do with, ‘How could my life have ended up here?’ Only that doesn’t really capture it, even. I just got lost in my head. I slept very deep. And I woke up late the next morning. You were all having pancakes.”

No, seriously – what was that clank? I’d opened the drawer and seen the phones.

But below that was another drawer.

Distracted though I am, I got her every word: pot beforehand, patchy sleep, deep sleep, late wake.

"I know you were stoned, but that wasn't a new thing. Is it possible that he...slipped you something?" I venture.

"I don't know for sure."

"And you don't remember anything else from that night?"

She shakes her head.

Hold on. Was there not a slim opening in the bottom of the cell phone drawer? A little line that made visible the drawer below?

Was there a box in that drawer? Cardboard?

Bullets?

I stand up, eyes toward the wall. It threatens to consume me. Turn back toward her, know that we're both thinking the same thing, generally:

Out. Get out.

Yet we're only doubters. We have no info. Particularly me, who could be getting a fiction here.

"I wouldn't hate you for just one mistake, you know," I tell her.

"I didn't. I'm not making anything up."

And she's not. For she, unlike the others, speaks straight. Never tries to sound like Him.

I turn to the wall again: staleness. Back to her: anything but.

"It got in my mind 'cause I talked to Jed," I say.

Her expression changes. The sort of expression one gets when, say, a ceiling drops down on one.

"You talked to Jed?"

I nod. I feel better (as well as worse).

"But he took all the phones and computers," she goes.

So I fish into my pocket and show what I took back. Dangle its redness, a bloody wound within her sight.

"I went in his room before," I say.

And then I'm down on the floor again, facing her, trying to use my eyes as a magnet for hers. Her head's not still, though. Its crowded thoughts zig it here and zag it there.

"Matthew. You shouldn't have done that. Why--?" Her eyes away from mine.

"I didn't think I'd use it. But Jed's been calling. He knows we're going through with the plan."

A catch where her throat meets her mouth. "You told him?"

"He knew it was coming. He doesn't know where we are."

I put the phone in her lap, and though I don't know quite how, it's a way of telling her how much I love her.

The thickness of my face seems to double; it scrunches up and wrenches out tears.

"I'm looking at you, Jolie. And I don't know if I can never see you again."

"Oh, no."

"Maybe, inside of me, that's the part that wanted to get the phone."

"You can't do this. You can't talk like that."

My words come in starts on account of my crying: "Jed told me before that you guys had sex, and then I thought I was real angry, but then I wasn't angry because I thought that I cared. I cared about you, baby."

The door's not far behind me. Close enough to send over some warmth. It opens, He sees this, He hears this...His heart will snap.

She's yet to meet my gaze. Her lips tremble. They'd tremble more, harder, if she met it.

Then, as if the ceiling weren't enough, I bring the whole house down on her: "I can't leave here unless you come with me."

Her eyes draw closed, let liquid slip.

"You can't put that on me." Whispering.

"Yes, I can. If he can put stuff on you then I can, also."

Just like Jed said to me. Leader on me. Jed on me. Me on her. The human race.

When her eyes come open, they look at me, hard. I see red veins and get a click of shock.

"I feel like I don't know who you are."

Makes two of us. Me not knowing me, nor her.

Good thing you don't have to know someone to love them.

"But I feel...like..." she says, and I hope-so-deep it's something good, "if I stop seeing you, my heart will break."

Hope answered.

Her hands in mine. Palms clammy yet perfect. We melt.

Eighty-Seven

Last Day – 3:13PM: UNSCHEDULED REVOLT

We're in the bathroom, now, together.

She hands me my phone and I want to hold her.

It's like the moment when you first get naked with someone, me showing her the bathroom. Yes, I know, she's seen it before, but never with me and my aims and my phone.

Sharing with her a new side.

Even as, through the window, I see the sun losing some strength.

I lock the door, turn on the sink, and do the other thing...

Only this time when I do it, I know exactly what I want to say.

Jed answers: "Matthew."

Statement-not-question.

"Just you, Jed," I say to him, my body relaxing for this moment alone. "No other people, do you understand?"

Jolie, I see, is rocking from side to side. Makes my body crunch up all over again.

"I do understand," he tells me, and right now I like him. Hopefully not just because he's taking orders.

"I can't have you lying to me. We don't want to see all of you right now."

"I know."

I look at Jolie. Then have to look away, no choice.

"We have dinner at five," I tell him. "We're gonna spend some time talking, and then the thing happens right at six."

"I'm walking out the door right now," Jed says. "You tell me where to go and I'll go there."

"You're not," I say, weak enough to disappear, "too far from here. You can be here for sure by five-thirty."

"Five-thirty, good. Just point the way."

I wake up, come back. Full force: heart and nerves. Jolie seems to flash with greater color. "We'll find a way to get outside, and you meet us at the end of the driveway. I'll grab anybody who wants to come. Do not - approach - the house."

"Okay, right, got it, I won't. The driveway."

"You have a van, you said?"

"A van, I do, yes."

I eye her again. Say, "Hang on a second."

Jed: "Go 'head."

I put the phone against the wet cloth covering my chest.

"You can do this, right?" I ask her. "You can do this with me?"

There's no pause. Her head's made to nod. I put the phone back to my ear and say, "Jed, we're still near Santa Barbara. We've gone to Summerland."

Eighty-Eight

Edgar Pike's Journal
June, 2010

Some gushes are more urgent than other gushes. The urge to make love is stronger than the urge to write. It blocks out the sky. It's all I need. That's my only remaining gush. If they stopped needing leadership, I wouldn't even speak anymore. It'd be love and hum. Bodies plus hum.

Yet I do have knowledge that I'm weak. Because the real philosopher would take the hum and not the gush. In other words, the real philosopher would find a way to discard the body.

Eighty-Nine

Last Day – 3:18PM

We exit the bathroom expecting a breath, but we clench up upon seeing Theodore.

As though it's his room. That's how settled he looks on the mattress.

He gets up when he sees us, though, and I ask him (phone: right pocket) what he's doing here.

He points at the bathroom: "What were *you* doing in *there*?"

No, no, no. I'm not having this. I step toward him, making his heels touch the mattress.

"You just come in on your own?"

"I heard you talking..."

Jolie behind me. I can't see her, but I know her well enough to know her arms are crossed.

"Talking about what?" I ask. "What are you saying, Theodore?"

He looks me up and down, his neck rhythm sloppy.

Then: "What's in your pocket?" he wants to know.

My hand goes into it, forms a shell around the phone.

"You knock before you come in here."

Jolie says, "Matthew."

And Theodore goes, "That was never a rule. I came in earlier, remem--?"

"Well, now it's a rule. You hear me? Now it's a rule."

Ninety

Edgar Pike's Journal
July, 2010

The legal system encompasses everything I find loathsome. Language used in service of constriction. Gray areas and mud all over the place. You get down to it, the laws don't matter. It's what the prosecutors decide.

Ninety-One

Last Day – 3:19PM

"Are you hiding something?" Theodore asks, displaying bemusement by way of his eyes alone. "Why are you being so aggressive?"

Nuh-uh. We don't go down here. Not on account of this fuck. "Am I really being aggressive?" I ask. "Or are you just a paranoid schizophrenic?"

Right then, I expect that he will grab me.

Only right then, as it happens, we're all grabbed by a shriek.

From downstairs.

Ninety-Two

Edgar Pike's Journal
September, 2009

This just occurred to me! I haven't thought about it in 20 years!

It was New Year's Eve. I lived up north, in Frisco, then (does anybody still use that word?). I was alone for the evening. Couldn't get a date, which meant my legs -- especially my upper legs -- were burning hard and hot. I wanted to put myself in someone.

I was credible then, even though I was young. I sold suits. (For me, it's always been sales -- even now.) I got up at the same time every morning. I called my mother and we'd have laughs.

But in 1989, ringing in 1990, I was walking down the street with my hands in my pockets when I saw a group of youngsters (college) walking toward me, laughing. Pretty girls and nice, upright boys. I grabbed one of the boys and screamed and threw him down on the sidewalk and yelled, "YOU MOTHERFUCKER!"

I did this! I don't know why. I don't even think he was scared! They were laughing after, as they walked away, like it was a cool thing to happen.

I never did anything like that afterward.

Ninety-Three

Last Day – 3:20PM

Within moments, it's me, Jolie, and Theodore by the upstairs railing overlooking the foyer.

The foyer, right now, looks like a stage, which is fitting since Beth is in it, walking around, tears in her eyes, hands sometimes in her hair, breaking every item she can find.

Given what The Leader did before we came, finding anything at all is a tall order. Regardless, she plucks a mirror from the wall and shatters it on the floor, endangering the eyes of Cathleen, who's a foot behind her, trying her best to stop this.

Also, there's this vase that The Leader's always liked, positioned on the floor beside the stairs. Beth picks it up above her head and smashes it against the floor.

The Leader's in sight, and in shock – not far from Cathleen.

And what Beth is doing isn't nearly as compelling as what she's yelling:

"I'm just asking you for this one thing. For this *one fucking thing*!"

Phrases come to mind here, among them "out of control" and "holy fucking shit!"

"Sweetheart," Cathleen says, reaching out a hand that doesn't dare to touch Beth, "you're going to have to calm down, so we can--"

"Get the hell away from me. Okay? This doesn't concern you."

So The Leader, whom it most assuredly concerns, says, "Beth...."

He, too, reaches in Beth's direction. She swipes His touch away like it's an insect.

Doing my best Calmest Man In The World impression, I ask them what's going on.

Cathleen looks up at us, seeming embarrassed, as though somehow this could possibly be her fault.

"She wants to call her mother," Cathleen explains.

My hand chokes the phone in my pocket.

The Leader tracks Beth out of the foyer. We hear a wood chair rattle across the floor. After a moment, they return.

"Beth," He says, "please. Come back to me now."

She turns back His way and shrieks her lungs out. These aren't soap opera actress shrieks; they actually resonate: "It's a goddamn minute. I've given you three fucking years of my life, and you can't just give me a *minute*?!"

"I'm afraid I can't allow it," He says. "I've expressed this to you already, and I'll continue expressing it to you."

"I won't say anything to her about where we are!" Beth's face defines redness. "I swear it."

"I'm not concerned about that," He goes.

"Then What Are You Concerned About?" The whole house, shuddering.

"Beth. The rules were clearly communicated to you when you got here, and you accepted them."

"I don't give a shit about the rules! Isn't that why we left the world out there? Because of the rules?"

"Let me tell you something about the rules out there. They're meant to disempower us, to keep us down, to tear away at all that is good and pure about each and every single one of us. And I--"

"How is that different from you not letting me speak to my mom? Tell me."

She lacks Jed's finesse, but she has a point.

The Leader just looks at her, no answer forming.

And I've got problems here. I'm voting against Beth. 'Cause if He tries to come upstairs and get a phone--

"Please," she says, gathering up some specks of calmness. "It's a phone call."

The Leader keeps on looking at her. If I'm not mistaken, that is love on His face. Or at least some affection for a being whom He likes banging.

Jolie steals a glance at me; I steal one back.

Both of us thinking: *phone.*

"Only for a minute," He says.

Beth leaps toward Him with a speed that implies violence. Only her leap concludes with an impassioned hug.

Now Theodore's eyeing me anew. Clowns to the left of me, jokers--

The Leader ends their hug. Eyes the steps. Starts to walk.

As I do, too. Toward the steps from the other direction.

"Wait here," He says, causing my belly to sizzle. "I'll get a phone for you."

Stepping downward, I look at Him: "What's going on?"

On His way up, He pauses. I think that I may have to end this here. Push Him down the steps when He gets closer. Murder. Not at all something I feel prepared for, but possibly a walk in the park compared to being caught.

"I'm allowing Beth a phone call," He explains, the epitome of officiousness. "Is that okay with you?"

Rather than re-explain His own rules to Him, rather than make a basic point about fairness, rather than warn Him that if He allows one call He may have to allow eight, I say, "Sure."

His eyes darken.

"I mean, of course," I say. "Just -- don't trouble yourself coming up. I'll get one for you, Master."

He's conducting a study of my face. It goes on a bit longer than one might expect.

"Do you know where I keep the phones?" He asks.

I blink. Once, twice, stop myself before the third. Each time my lids come down, I'm in hell.

"Uh. No," I say.

And now we're two guys staring at each other. The only sound is Beth's lungs straining.

"Bedside table in my room. Top drawer."

Does He see my pocket? Can He see through my pocket? Will He pull me backwards-downwards when I turn?

None of the above, apparently.

When I get a new phone, I replace my own.

But that doesn't mean I'm goddamn checking back in.

Ninety-Four

Edgar Pike's Journal

September, 2009

Matthew's a stupid child.

Ninety-Five

Last Day – 3:33PM

Again, in our room, she and me. For the last time.

Before dinner is The Eternity Chant. Then food that we'll have to fight to swallow. Then-

"You have to save me," Jolie says. "If he catches on. Like if I start talking stupid."

We're holding each other. Upright. On our feet. Door locked beside us.

"I save you, you save me," I say. "Besides, it's okay. He expects us all to talk weird."

"Okay, yeah, right." Then she asks: "What if Jed doesn't make it?"

This has crossed my mind, as well. Car accidents happen, even amidst rescue missions (and especially when you drive like Jed). And lateness happens, too, for no goddamn reason whatsoever.

Earliness, as well, in terms of The Leader electing to push us along faster.

I picture us running out the back door, but our feet would be no match for The Leader's car, and I'd like to give the others a chance to join.

My expectation: Beth would come. Michael would stay. Theodore: stay. Cathleen, Paul, and Susan may as well be dead already. The Leader: I don't know...I'm putting my chips on stay.

Inward sarcasm as danger looms.

That means me, Jolie, and Beth, or one-third. Not horrible, although I'd like to get all of us, Him included.

Could I pull that off? Could I make like Jed? Start talking all slick and get the Big Man to bend?

Not likely, you want to know my opinion.

But to issue them a choice is a step. It's something. It might end up amounting to a handful of sand, but I'll take that over my own corpse.

There is one thing – one single thing – that I can do to tip the odds of a clean sweep in my favor, but it's too ridiculous to even contemplate. Certainly above my pay grade.

I could...

No, never mind. You don't have half the needed guts.

"No matter what," I say to her. "We walk out the door. Don't look back. No matter what, okay?"

"Okay, yeah, okay."

"Like the guy in the story Jed told, right?" My "right" isn't nearly as lacerating as Jed's. "We say 'why not?' and walk out."

She starts to cry. Even if I don't live, I'm glad I got to share that with somebody. And who better?

We kiss. Two mouths open. I pull away first.

I say, "At dinner, I'm gonna tell everyone that we're going."

"Yeah, okay."

"I'm serious."

"I know you are."

"Everybody gets the option to come. We don't care what he does or says."

"We don't."

"We don't care what he does or says."

She nods. It's a crap plan. The worst, but it's all we've got.

"Right around five-thirty," I go, "I'm going to ask permission to speak. Whether he grants it or not, I explain it. It'll take ten seconds."

She moves away from me, does some rocking. Front to back, beats her torso's rear against the wall.

"There's no question we can do this. Just think about afterwards."

I'm liking the way I sound: some kind of leader.

"No, I'd rather -- I gotta stay in the present right now, you know?" she says.

I nod. Right, the present. The Leader would've known that.

We eye each other.

"Matthew, kiss me more, okay?" she says.

And so I do.

Ninety-Six

Edgar Pike's Journal
July, 2011

I'll burn this journal. Yet I do want to say in ink that I never raped anyone. That is truth. Why deny it to myself? I wouldn't. What I did in private with them was wanted on their parts. Laura once said I knew her better than she knew herself, which was true. And is now. She and Allison lived through rapes in their minds -- and live through them again in their memories -- but that was a delusion penned in chaos.

Ninety-Seven

Last Day – 4PM: ETERNITY CHANT

Throughout the chant, I think not of eternity. Despite the concept's elephantine proportions, I manage to push it away.

Somehow the thought of Beth's mother is enough to take its place.

What is the opposite of eternity called?

What could that phone call have possibly been like?

Saying goodbye for no goddamn reason. Just 'cause a megalomaniac who killed a baby got an idea in His head.

We're all on the floor. All nine of us: The Leader joins. He's in the center; we surround Him like satellites.

Together, a little solar system.

And we chant (you saw it coming): "Eternity..."

Over and over again, we chant it. It's the kind of thing where, just when you expect it to get wrapped up, it goes on for another hundred miles.

"Eternity.

"Eternity.

"Eternity.

"Eternity.

"Eternity..."

Jolie's hand in mine. My hand around hers.

I am your protector, I think.

And Beth's mom: I am your protector, too.

And all of these people: I am your savior.

Hear me!

“Eternity...”

Love me!

“Eternity...”

Know I’m right.

Know that I’m just a boy, but I’m here to save you.

Ninety-Eight

Edgar Pike's Journal

August, 2011

I couldn't take prison. My career was an enemy to me. Prison would be my murderer.

Ninety-Nine

Last Day – 5PM: DINNER

Five's here. The sun's wilting. The whole day a flash.

Whenever, in life, you arrive at a point that you've been building up to, there's always a sense of banality about it. You realize, when you get there, that you're still just you. Same eyes, same senses. And in front of you is still just the world.

Only the context provides it with emotion.

That sense of banality tends to fade whenever you actually do whatever you have to. It may fade for worse or it may fade for better, but before long the situation gets ignited, turns into a heady thing.

Every book report I ever gave.

Every girl I ever finally kissed.

Every time I finally told someone off. (Only once, that. My dad. The kitchen. Orange light from outside. And I hope my words make him sting till the day he dies.)

And here at dinner, right at this moment, there's that plain, beige, ordinary lilt. Fuck, we're just nine people at dinner. The Leader may have stuffed the situation fat with notions of unity consciousness and mind-out-of-time-ness, but no such notions have ever stopped a dining room from being just that.

Which is not to say that I couldn't soil my chair.

Not to say, as well, that Jolie's fear isn't as obvious as the sky.

I'm next to Him, near the head. To my right is she.

On every plate is chicken or fish, dead animals put to greater use than He intends to put us to. Every glass has in it juice or wine, also, but no one's touching a thing.

Bearing more of our attention than the food are the knives.

Nine of them. Center table. Aligned in a sparkling row.

"When the day began," The Leader says, not bothering to rise, "as I said to Matthew, I wanted it to go quickly. But as we sit here, I realize that it went too quickly even for me."

He smiles. Everybody but us two smile back.

About Beth, I begin to have my doubts. She beams.

He says, all windy, "If it's okay with everybody, I'd like to go around the table and collect your final thoughts within this realm..."

The Leader's hands levitate above the table.

He goes on: "Now, if anybody doesn't want to participate, don't worry about it for a moment, just say, 'Pass.'"

Sounds of breath at this table like you wouldn't believe.

He says, "Since Cathleen prepared this beautiful meal, I think we'll all agree that she should go first."

Cathleen smiles and pushes her hair back from her shoulders. All eyes but mine land upon her.

I eye my knife. Not the suicide one, the dinner one. Could I do what I thought of? Is it not that absurd?

Cathleen says, “Um, I guess you won’t hear anything too original from me. I’m a better cook than I am a public speaker.”

Some laughs are generated. Just a cheery old band of pre-suicides.

“But I guess,” Cathleen continues, “I’d just like to say that I love you all, and that these couple of years among you have been so, so wonderful, and as I look around at all your faces, I find myself bursting with anticipation, because I can’t wait to see what you look like for real, outside of your shells.”

The Leader smiles upon recognizing His own words. He raises His wine-filled glass, presents her with a robust “Hear, hear.”

We all pick up our glasses and repeat: “Hear, hear.”

“A very impressive speaker after all!” He says, a ghostwriter praising the author of record.

Cathleen grins and tilts her eyes downward.

“And who would like to follow Cathleen?”

Jolie looks at me. I look back. Her eyes are like “NOW.”

But Theodore goes, “I would just like to say, ‘Thank you.’”

So all heads turn to face him.

And Theodore says, “I want to of course echo what Cathleen said about loving everybody, but I want to also say, ‘Thanks for everything.’ All of you have made me feel welcome in a way that I didn't know was possible. And your generosity has continued up to the very end."

Then he turns to The Leader, and, while keeping the outward peace, raises a kind of raging hell: "And I have to say, I'm so honored to have been selected to make the transition right before you."

The Leader, unchanged, nods.

My heart gets smashed.

"I'm honored, as well," The Leader lies, suddenly staring me down via His peripherals.

I tighten up so much that my body could stand without my will.

Theodore then turns to me, and although he's merely speaking, each word from him hits me as though it's yelled:

"And of course Matthew is owed thanks for that, for sacrificing his own place in the order."

His piece said, Theodore looks back at The Leader.

But The Leader, ignoring him, now looks right at me.

I get, now, why Jolie likes to rock back and forth. My chair's just shy of creaking.

"I..." The Leader is searching. "...wouldn't have it any other way, Theodore."

The Leader's gaze, as He says this, is fixed on me. Surrounds me. Makes itself my home.

Then: "Who goes next?" asks The Leader.

Still: His eyes: All me.

I look right back and think about the front lawn. Should have walked away: naked boy. Gone into town. Explained.

Been on the news. A bizarre folk hero.

Entirely oblivious to the Ascending tension, Beth leans forward in her seat and says:

"I think everybody's hitting the nail on the head. You're not only beautiful...and filled with love...and deserving of thanks, as Theodore said, but you're also so much fun to play with."

Giggles abound. Briefly, The Leader looks at Beth, sparkles in His eyes.

"You all," she goes, "have such nice skin and such sweet lips and it's been so nice with those of you who I've touched and laid with and had a chance to explore. And beyond all that..." This part for The Leader. "...I just wanted to thank you for bending the rules a little for me today. That showed great courage, and my respect for you has risen to a height I never thought possible. Thank you."

Nearly everyone here is a beam of delight.

But only nearly.

The Leader, discarding Beth, goes and eyes me some more. Jolie, too, part of the time.

Michael chimes in: "Um. I want to say that this has been a real transition for me. I know we've done a lot of serious work, but I'm happy Beth mentioned how much fun it is, also. Because it really has been spirited and free. And even when we're not in the best of moo—"

The Leader asks me, “What the fuck is wrong with you?”

Like lightning, I grab my dinner knife and press it against His throat.

“You fucking bastard!” I explode.

In my stomach, right-then, is His gun. Any more pressure and it'll cut right into me.

My heart, right now, is in jailbreak mode.

“You really want to try that, you fucking prick?” The Leader asks.

I say to Him, “Go 'head. Shoot me. SHOOT ME! You fucking murderer! Show them what a murderer you are!”

He pauses. No doubt His penis has crawled inside of His body. His eyes, full of motion, are absorbing my point.

Everybody at the table is suspended in time. All of them seem on the verge of speaking-screaming-rising, but no one does a thing.

“You tell these fucking people we are not going through with this,” I say.

Hey, I told you how out there the whole plan was.

His gun: harder. Deep in my belly. It's on its way to my spine.

“Matthew, you are a good boy. Don't do this. You're frightened. Don't make me hurt you.”

“All you've WANTED is to hurt me!”

“No.”

“Yes. You're a savage.”

Near to the blade, His throat is red.

I say, “You've motherfucked my whole goddamn mind. All of us.”

Beth cries, “Matthew!”

I turn to her, head fast: “Do you never want to see your mom again?”

Back to Him, though. Can't stick 'round for her reaction.

“I so much as hear,” I say, “that trigger squeak, and I will open your neck and we'll all live.”

“Matthew...” He's running low on breath.

“'Cause with you gone I'm thinking they'll all wake the fuck up, and see this circus for what it is.”

Jolie, to my right, is a creature of shakes. Somehow, though, I'm getting hard vibes from her, and they're loaded up tight with information.

Love.

She loves me.

She does so full.

And seeing me like this turns her on.

Why doesn't Jed walk in so he can see, too?

The Leader's blood's dripping. He speaks to me with impressive composure: “We had something beautiful here. You've scarred it and you've disgraced yourself.”

I'm a monster, roaring: “You've disgraced all of us! We're human beings! We're not your fucking play things.”

Gun moving. Trigger?

I press in the knife.

“Call it off. Go home. Face your destiny.”

Then, from His red face: “I fucked your girlfriend, all right? I FUCKED THAT PUSS—”

Tight thunder from inside. Lower back's blown out in a slapping charge.

I hear a hard and masculine scream—

Then whizzing at me, feral, comes Death. Petting, throttling, stomping me. Diagonal mind and eyes a blankness—

He's up: *sudden.* Ascendant. I blink-blink-blink, my weak cheeks jumping, waiting for Him to shoot me again. With each bend of my pulse, my stomach chomps itself—

Jolie's up, also. Arched over me; her hair my own forest. Both eyes turned liquid, her love in a drip.

The Leader, I see, has a straightened elbow.

PAUL:

His whole face, previously pale, cracks into a redness: A rose in fast-forward bloom. His hands tried to cover his face before the bullet smashed it. They're up as he falls, or Ascends, and I realize despite a billion brain cells of resistance that He intends to kill us all--

CATHLEEN:

She's up on her bare feet. They slap-slap the hardwood as she runs with elegance. I licked her once, before Jolie. Thought her skin a thing of purity and softness, but—

The Leader spikes hot steel through her back. Hundreds of miles per hour from gun to body. Her right lung a geyser split between her chest and throat. The wood floor reaches up and smacks her. Colossal knocks as her knees land, then her chin and then the rest of her--

THEODORE:

His head's been overtaken by a broadening scream. My hand, which weighs a thousand pounds, travels upward through the universe to touch my belly, which is hot/too hot and pouring out a sugar-sweet mess. His jowls tight, The Leader paces to Theodore. The scream – attempting to release that ill mind – holds the man's mouth open as wide as possible. The Leader jams the gun right in there, scrapes the roof of Theodore's mouth. A steel crack splinters Theodore's mind. Spray of schizophrenic tissue out the back of his skull. I'm being dragged. Jolie's arms show the strength which she till-now has kept inside--

SUSAN:

“Take me away now, Master!” she yells. She's the only one still sitting, across from Theodore's empty seat. Never before have I heard her so loud. Her banality has left her (a moment prior to her life). Ascension! Thunder-crack! The bullet splits her chest with mad-gorilla force. The Leader's eyes, unblinking, possess jungle-like chaos--

BETH:

Tiptoes up behind The Leader. (Enter stage right.) When He turns to face her, His eyebrows crumple. (Still no blinking, though.) Jolie drags me, heaving. Her chest engaged in an orgasmic inhale, Beth asks to get it "straight through my heart." He pauses. Nods, then. Takes aim again, but she's not far away enough for Him to stretch His arm. Regardless, she shakes her head (eyes gripped by a hunger), and narrows the little space between them. "Let me bleed on you," she breathes and breathes. A blink at last. He recalls He's our master. "You sexy bitch" comes out of Him, so garbled you can hardly hear it. He point-blank fires, punctures her breastplate. Her heart spills outward. Charred blackness, briefly. (Standing ovation.) A legit assassination, hers. His hand and face are stone, then--

MICHAEL:

He's been looming to The Leader's left. Body language tentative; one hand hovering with a finger shy of pointing. The Leader turns. Jolie's got me center-room now: foyer visible. "Maybe you should..." This is Michael reasoning -- not saying, "Why not?" He receives a clean shot. Forehead caves in/rear skull spits out. His mismatcher mind replaced by silence. Once on the floor, his body writhes, not having wanted it. Jolie's hands scrunch my cloth. She's a hundred feet above me, sobbing. Fingers scratching sometimes. Floor's all ice, and it's near to burning me. I skate past the rears of The Leader's calves—then into the foyer—then--

JED!

He just walked in, in three dimensions. As though he never went away. "Special Appearance By..." He sports a burnt-wood rifle; front door's still in the process of opening behind him. He and The Leader are two ancient animals, trading screams for greetings. I'm iced by tiles. Jed rams out a shot: The Leader's shoulder's a dark spray. A chunk of Him twirls upward, cartwheels. It's not His gun arm, though. He aims back, *hits* back. Bullet makes wind as it tears by Jolie. It's like, for a micro-second, Jed sees what's coming. Handsome face meeting worst possible fate. Jed's eye socket pukes and blossoms. He falls and crumbles, should've waited outside. Which is where we are. Blackness now covering the whole big sky. The Leader runs toward us, shoulder shedding--

JOLIE & ME:

We're out in the cold and dark. Night-grass flooding up toward me, its scent spiking into my nose. My dying legs petting its perfect coolness. From His mouth comes a Roar. He's parted with language, is a primitive Thing. Jed's car's got its lights on. If he left the keys in, we could have a chance--

The girl drags me in that direction. Smell of my blood so strong I bet she can taste it. My mid-torso a knot tied in many directions. “No bullet for you!” He screams at her. Jed took it for her; he's good like that. She grinds on, strength-less, working only from will. He's gun-less, I see. But He wields a blade. After eyeing us both for a breathless moment, He breaks into a goofy but horse-fast run. She drops me and my head tornadoes. I'm a million feet below the ground, existing amidst bugs and red mud, closing in on the Center of the Earth. When He gets to her, He swings at her. Draws steel heat across her flesh. The teeth of the blade part arms, then breasts. Clean lines for wounds: opening, pausing, then spilling blood. Out here her human juice looks black.

But she's long known the touch of unwanted hands. Her instinct lever pulls and her own arms rise. Pair of fists like stone cores. With slicing force, the girl goes at Him. Cracks His temples. Works to crunch His nose. Her human noise all 'round His head. Flesh connections dull yet thick -- Populated!

When her fists spring open, her long nails dig. He roars again, but the pitch is higher. His eyes, I glimpse, are sparkling red. Then: His cheeks are scrunched open, rosy in two shades: one from blood on the inside, other from blood gone visible. Starved for a move, He leaps upward, landing down on her. Knife with a moonlight twinkle as it's dropped.

She falls/they fall/they flood my sight. We make a triple-decker crunch. Her nails continue with His eyes. His hands slop their way to her neck. My own hand, all million pounds of it, presses upward, seeking His throat. The three of us, grunting. I've got His Adam's apple, finally. It's a tight clench, devoid of any air. My fingers twist it while pushing inward. Jolie's blood, I feel, is mixing with mine, though I've got way fucking more to go around.

“You...mother...fucker,” I exhale upward, each syllable something I have to work for.

“Be over in a second,” He squeaks, strangling Jolie as He tries in vain to pull back from me.

Tug-of-war: I yank His Adam's apple toward us. Hoping to hear His esophagus crack. Hear tight gargles instead, just behind His neck flesh. His eyes, so bloody, are without any sharpness. And His snapped throat seems to be raging for just one cough. That's it, though. He can't get air. His grip around Jolie's neck starts to melt. We watch Him, curious. I haven't been this close to Him since the night they all left. She: not since the night He raped her. Fitting that He's dying on top of a woman. I realize with alarming simplicity that that's all He ever wanted. Would've realized it back in the house, but was too busy getting steel blown through my guts.

Impatient, Jolie reaches upward. She shoves her whole hand inside of His mouth, then reaches around and causes Him to produce an insect bark. She's fingering His air-hole, and I'm guessing there are at least two digits in it. She keeps on pressing for several seconds. He's trying to ventilate, but His brain's not in it. By now it's just something His body's doing.

My thoughts all dizzy, I regard the shrieking craziness of seeing a being so lethal reduced to a gargling mammal.

We're the only two breathing, now, I think. She rolls Him off of us. I expect to breathe easier, but my lungs pin me downward. I think it might be check-out time. Something like euphoria's crushing my head. Broken stomach seems real far away. I'd think of dandelions if I could remember what they look like, or anything else for that matter...

Her. I remember her. The fact that she's right beside me helps. If I could speak, I'd say that I'll never forget her. How much I love her. And that I know, whether she knows it or not, that she loves me totally. That's been my special gift to her. As well as the life she'll walk away with.

I try to touch her. She's leaning over me now, breasts swinging downward, breath reaching me but words retreating backwards. Weird words; funneling shapes; going nowhere. Meant for me, though, I'm pretty sure.

Can't touch her. Can hardly think of doing so. Can only seem to touch what's above her: all that plush and sparkling darkness. It's getting realer. As is everything...But the place for me is still with her. And I try to see her. Don't want to never see her again...

But I go, and she's a crying girl on the grass. All alone beneath the massive night. Never to know my touch nor hear my words, never to share my bed nor be my wife.

****

So sorry, baby. I did my best. Hopefully I'll see you around. In the meantime, though, may you make a good life. And may love find you and hold you till the day glows pink and total with its might.

Author's Bio

Eric Shapiro is a writer and filmmaker. Called "the next Philip K. Dick" by author Kealan Patrick Burke, Shapiro is the author of six critically acclaimed fiction books, among them the novella "It's Only Temporary" (2005), which appeared on Nightmare Magazine's list of the Top 100 Horror Books, and numerous short stories published in anthologies alongside work by H.P. Lovecraft, Ray Bradbury, Stephen King, Chuck Palahniuk, and many others. His nonfiction articles have been published on The Daily Dot, Ravishly, and The Good Men Project. His first feature film, "Rule of 3" (2010), won awards at the Fantasia International Film Festival and Shriekfest, and had its U.S. premiere at Fantastic Fest. His second feature film, "Living Things" (2014), was endorsed by PETA (People For The Ethical Treatment of Animals) and distributed by Cinema Libre Studio. In 2015, he won the 19th Annual Fade In Award for Thriller Screenplays. He was a founding partner of Ghostwriters Central, a writing and editing firm which has received positive notices from The Wall Street Journal, Consumers Digest, and the TV program "Intelligence For Your Life." Eric has edited works published on The Huffington Post and Forbes, as well as two Bram Stoker Award-nominated novels. He lives in Northern California with his wife, Rhoda, and their two sons.

Also by Eric Shapiro:

Short story collections
Short of a Picnic

Nonfiction
Ass Plus Seat

Novels
Red Dennis

Novellas
It's Only Temporary
Days of Allison
Strawberry Man
Love & Zombies

Printed in Dunstable, United Kingdom

80602776R00133